GOAT ROPE

a Charlemagne file by
K.A. Bachus

Published in Bangor, Maine, United States of America
Contact the publisher at info@charlemagnefiles.com

Visit: https://www.charlemagnefiles.com

Cover by Marigold Faith

CHARLEMAGNE FILE TIMELINES

Short Story Collection
A Lighter Shade of Night,
mid 60s to early 70s

Novels
Trinity Icon, early 70s
Cetus Wedge, early 80s
Brevet Wedge, nine months later
Lion Tamer, five months later
State of Nature, early 90s
Vory, a year later
Swallow, five weeks later
Quiet Move, late 90s
Goat Rope, 1999

CONTENTS

Author's Note

By design, the racist language used by Charlemagne's targets in this book jars modern sensibilities. The author hopes the truthful depiction of an ugly worldview in a story otherwise meant to divert and entertain will alert those who do not hold such views to think again before forming alliances with those who do.

PROLOGUE

Montreal, October 1970

So kill him, Rusty Tobrin wanted to say. He paused to rearrange his words, to make them more palatable to ensure compliance.

"If the Canadian minister were to die under your care, shall we say, the authorities would be more willing to negotiate for the life of the British diplomat, would they not?"

He observed the young Mountie carefully, tracing the thought he had implanted as it developed behind his eyes. Their friendship—or what this agent thought was a friendship—was too new to risk by giving a direct order. Use suggestions only, Rusty's revered teacher and mentor, Ignaty, had stressed, though he would never be so impertinent as to call him Ignaty out loud. The man was now more powerful than ever in the First Directorate.

Give his thoughts a path to follow without posting arrows on the trees, Ignaty had advised.

"There might be other ways to convince them the FLQ is serious, but..." Rusty left the rest of the sentence to be completed by Antoine's own thoughts, shook his head slightly to indicate hopelessness, watched for the dawn of understanding in his eyes, and pulled an envelope out of his pocket at just the right time, taking care to activate the tiny camera in his tie pin by pressing the switch behind it as the young man gratefully accepted the payment he had come to depend upon.

1

It may have been this conversation or similar conversations by officers senior to him who controlled another agent among the more extreme inner members of the FLQ, or perhaps it was a natural progression in the logic of violent political action—no matter which—the minister died. The government reacted with predictable extremist measures, further demonstrating the decadent impotence of liberal democracy. Rusty liked to think he had a hand in it. Damage done: the Canadian military diverted to internal affairs, and NATO weakened. There couldn't be a better outcome. He and his colleagues celebrated with quiet jubilation—and vodka.

After a few weeks, Antoine brought him more intelligence, setting the ambitious young Rusty on the path of what he hoped would be a brilliant career. He indulged in fantasies of sitting behind Ignaty Slavin's desk in Moscow while still young enough to enjoy the perks that came with the job.

A turncoat among the FLQ was cooperating with the fascist authorities, Antoine told him. The authorities had custody of the traitor, having suspended habeas corpus, but that was no matter.

What to do? He surveyed the man—young, fit, greedy, ideologically ambiguous. Antoine had inside information, an accurate eye, and access to a police rifle.

And Rusty had Antoine.

ONE

Montreal 1999

B rother,
You know I'm yer most committed and valuable agent of our angry God. I know yer his anointed. You said don't be noticeable, stand down till you can give us our assignments. I'm the best fighter of all of us in this here cleansing work for the cause and a helluva lot more obedient than all the others, now that Sal's dead. Nothing stops me doing what you say. You said we gotta help our Canadian brethren in their struggles for the white race, and you know I'm fully on board with that. I stand on my record.

That said, I'm reporting an incident. Minor, of course, but yer probably gonna hear about it. I aim to tell you the facts involved so's to alert you about a small possible problem that'll probably never come up, but you never know. Right?. You like us to report the truth, and you always take it into account before you react to a problem, even when nobody's at fault. I get the need for order and discipline in the ranks. I always agree with your decisions, even when I'm the one that needs correcting, and even when a criminal from a degenerate race is the real cause of that there difficulty.

I was just walking, that's all, heading for St. Catherine Street through a small park, maybe five hundred by three hundred yards a couple blocks west of it. There was some woods on one side and a big street on the other. Some benches was there, and some bushes. Nobody was around, but then I saw this guy, a coon so black he were almost blue, lollygagging on this here bench. He took up the whole seat so's nobody else could sit there, and I knew, I just knew, no decent white person would want ever to sit there again after this. It enraged me.

I kicked him in the shin, told him to move his black ass. He didn't have no business being there, I said. I pointed at a dumpster behind the bushes. Go hang out where you belong, I says.

Can you believe it? He starts jabbering away at me in that French lingo they use so much around here. It could've been Swahili or some such shit for all I know, except he has enough respect for a white man that I hear him say the word mon-sewer that the shopkeepers on Guy Street use all the time.

I kick him again cuz he ain't moving. I scream pretty loud, trying to make him see he's got no business there, when he stands up and starts hollering, too. He's a big boy, and he raises a fist like in an uppercut and holds it under my nose, and then he's got the nerve to look me in the eye, spouting his gibberish.

It were automatic, really, the fruit of all the great training the brotherhood give me. Anyway, I drew my weapon cuz I didn't have no choice.

So I fire, and he falls down dead with his head in a flower bed and a hole in his chest spouting blood and making a mess of the flowers. I don't know what kind. They was purple with white bits on the edges, but now the ones that ain't crushed has red spatters all over them.

Our mission is way too important to let things like this mess it up, so I think for a minute, then scan around me. People is running up but still a block away. I wheel round to disappear the other way and run into this bitch out of nowhere. I could have taken care of her, too, but a couple guys was running down the sidewalk to the right, no more than fifty yards, and the ones behind me was gaining, so I dodged left, jumped the bushes, and lost myself in a patch of woods long enough to come out on a busy pathway at the other side, pretending like nothing happened.

I got a little notebook and a pen at a newsstand on the street and will drop this in the dead drop you told me to use in emergencies. I remember the signal, so I hope you get it. I ain't got time to do any coding shit, but who's gonna know, right? I'll keep low for a day or two and watch the news before I try making contact again.

The bitch is about five-five, slim, not old, but not young, either. Her hair's brown and tied back in a ponytail. Eyes are brown, too. I don't think she's entirely white. Probably some kind of mulatto with high cheekbones and funny eyes, like a chink. She were wearing a dark blue or maybe black tank top with a design around the bottom, pink and green and blue, and khaki shorts and maybe sandals. She'll be easy to find, though, because of this here little dog she had on a leash. It were real small, but not like one of them tea-cup dogs. About ten pounds, maybe. Easy to spot, though. It's brown and white with big, stand-up ears. One of them rat dogs. Barked like crazy.

I'm sure the other guy you got coming can find her and eliminate the problem. She ain't young, maybe, but her face and body don't agree with the coupla grey streaks in her hair, so there's extra incentive if they need it.

Sincerely, *Smitty*

TWO

"I never liked the girl," Misha said as he sat in the seat facing Rimas. "I suspected she was dirty."

Rimas tore his dark blue eyes from the clouds below to look at his mentor as their jet turned downwind on its approach to Montreal. Soon, he would see Jade. He drew in his long legs to keep from hogging the space and brushed back the dark hair on his forehead. What was Misha talking about? Was he hinting Jade might be dirty? Impossible. They knew everything about her, even the double date her friends dragged her into last week. That guy was lucky he had no chance to kiss her. Rimas did not trust himself to let him live if he had.

He thought he had learned enough German in school, but after two years of living and working with Misha, the man's Austrian accent and occasional archaic word choices still mystified him. He needed clarification. It took only a puzzled look to get it.

Misha sighed as he re-fastened his seat belt and leaned back. His handsome face showed a light network of wrinkles competing with a few faded scars. "Not Jade, Rimas. Why must you think every mention of a woman refers to her? I told you the girl's name was Gloria, and Vasily did not believe me. Were you listening? It was 1971."

"Vasily? Do you mean the man who bought the pretty carpet in the corridor at home?"

"Yes. Gloria was one of the first American girls he spoke to. He had difficulty talking with women, but she had an easy manner, and he was able to speak in sentences. They met in a café on the street where we had set up surveillance of our target. It was the Rue de Montagne."

"In America?"

Misha's patient stillness reminded Rimas to try a little thinking. Funny how the man had the same manner when dealing with both lethal threats and ordinary stupidity.

Rimas nodded to show he understood. "In Montreal," he said. "But the girl was American?"

"She was. Vasily took every opportunity to meet American women even before that operation. It had become a new hobby of his. He wanted to collect them like figurines on a mantlepiece. They were always chipped or damaged or flawed in some way. Sometimes, the artist had been sloppy, making one too tall, another too slim."

Rimas remembered snippets of conversation heard here and there—no, not here, not operationally—at home, at Vasily's Carpet, where he could mind his own business with benevolent disinterest. He turned his head and narrowed one eye at Misha.

"Vasily married an American, didn't he? Just like you did."

Misha rolled his eyes, exasperated. "Yes. Just like me. The same American."

"Gloria?" Rimas never paid much attention to the relationships or personalities in Misha's gigantic house, but he knew he had never heard that name mentioned before. Was she an ex? Would Misha have an ex? Alive? He knew there had been an earlier wife who had been killed by enemies—Michael's mother. He was certain she was not called Gloria.

Misha covered his eyes with one hand and looked at him through the fingers.

"No. Alex," he hissed.

Rimas was still confused, though he recognized the name and could picture her presiding over the dining table, with soft brown curls and a dimpled smile—the only person with license to argue with Misha regularly. But further explanation would have to wait. His son, Michael, moved up the aisle, barking orders at the team as the jet began its final descent into Montreal.

"Rimas, haul that footlocker with the rifles up here now. I want everything ready to unload when we come to a stop on the ramp. Steve, wake up and give Sergei a hand."

The familiar chaos that always attended the beginning of an operation drove all questions about strange women in the past from Rimas's mind. He stacked one locker atop another while Michael took the seat he vacated. Shouldering his heavy duffel bag, he held a grab bar next to the door and anticipated the coming reunion with his beloved Jade. It had been months. Through a window to the left, he watched the ground swell to meet them, amazed at the patchwork of colors, a geometry in shades of green.

Father and son faced each other across a cloud-filled window on the other side of the cabin. Rimas turned to look at them as the clouds interfered with his view. Michael's hair was without grey and lighter than his father's, and he wore it shorter. Misha's royal blue eyes were striking, but his son's gaze contained more ice.

"Papa, do you think we will need the Škorpions?" said Michael, referring to the machine pistols in another locker.

Misha turned from his examination of the yellow and green quilt below them as the view cleared. "You have done very well these two years. Your judgment is flawless. Trust it. I do."

"I cannot believe you quit the game, Papa. I worry. Vasily…"

"I have not quit. I am operationally retired. Vasily only pretended he was normal until normality killed him. I am enjoying retirement too much to let that happen. I assure you I am armed; I will defend myself and the team if necessary, but please, do not assign me a specific task in your operation. It is bad enough your stepmother has required me to do her bidding. I will not take orders from you as well."

Rimas pretended not to listen, gluing himself to the window and the swelling size of the trees below him.

Michael shifted forward in his seat and lowered his voice. The engine noise would keep ordinary conversation private, but Rimas stood at the door, not quite far enough away.

"What reason did Alex give you, Papa?"

"She insists I created the problem and am morally bound to solve it. But what you want to ask me is how she induced me to bother with this. I had no choice. She threatened to come with us. After what happened in Florida, I cannot allow it. I will not have her injured like that again."

Michael raised the brows above his blue eyes with an ironic half-smile. "Just forbid her."

Misha grimaced, perhaps searching for a way to explain the hold they all knew the woman had on his heart. He never confessed any weakness, least of all one that revealed an emotional attachment, and Rimas was sure he would not divulge it now. At least not without torture. Maybe not even then.

Glancing again at the looming earth beyond the window next to him, Misha formed an answer."Do you trust your wife's medical judgment?"

"You know I do. I must. I know very little…"

Misha gave a slow nod. "Alex is not a surgeon, but she knows human character better than I do. She insists it must be done and I must do it."

Michael's eyes widened. "Your judgment of people is flawless, Papa. How can Alex be better? And how will you separate the two of them?"

Separate who? Rimas risked looking at them as tree-tops sped by beyond the cement runway.

"How will you find the tangos the Americans hired you to eliminate?" Misha asked his son.

The aircraft touched down as father and son locked their eyes in silent consternation. They would figure it out, no doubt, and Rimas would do as he was told. And Jade…?

And Jade.

Rimas searched the tarmac for her as they taxied to their parking spot.

THREE

S kosh pulled the Mercedes M-Class SUV forward onto the ramp and parked alongside the jet's cargo bay. Jade pulled up to the stairs in front of him. She drove the S-Class sedan requested by Charlemagne, the team of deadly operatives they were there to meet.

He shuddered. He knew the sedan meant something he wasn't going to like. The team had never requested two specific cars before. Even after Mack retired, his son, who used the game name Charlie, maintained the one-Mercedes tradition, though he opted for the more practical SUV. Skosh suspected one too many people were about to get off that airplane. He had an uncomfortable feeling Charlie's father, Mack, would be that one. The man was a legend among babysitters like Skosh, earning his game name because of his facility with a knife.

Skosh hated being proved right as he watched the man climb down the steps. Mack still held a cane but didn't use it on the stairs. He didn't even hold the handrail. Skosh remembered the sight of that bloody hip as he had helped hoist him onto the gurney. He remembered the screaming fight with Charlie. He remembered losing it. It was a miracle of modern medicine and Charlie's wife, the surgeon, that Mack could even stand on that leg, let alone take the stairs without holding on. Grudgingly, Skosh added the impossible standards of physical conditioning these guys maintained to his private 'miracle of' list.

At the bottom of the stairs, Mack handled the cane like a gentleman's affectation rather than a mobility tool for a man with a dodgy hip.

"He's coming to my passenger door." Jade's voice on the radio sparked a fresh set of misgivings about this op. "What should I do?"

"Unlock the door."

Skosh wanted to add 'you silly girl.' He wanted to tease her and jest with her and call her names, little sweet names just between them, names only he would be allowed to say to her. He set aside the fleeting thought, ruthlessly tamped it down before it could become the usual lead weight in the depths of his psyche.

I can't have her, he reminded himself as he unlocked the SUV doors and climbed out to open the tailgate for the team to stow their weapons in the back.

Steve Donovan had a few strands of early grey mixed at the temples. He wore his thick brown hair a bit too long, a belligerent reaction to his military past, a personal statement that he was entirely civilian now, despite a vocabulary rich in the use of acronyms and f-words. He shared these generously in conversation—if you could call it that—with his fellow delinquent, Sergei, whose sandy hair showed no signs of grey. Skosh felt a ping of jealousy. His temples had more little white strands against the black than he liked. He blamed the team and the nature of their work. Skosh and the delinquents (his pet name for them) were all of an age, clustered just under forty. Not old enough to be completely serious, but too old to be forgiven their screw-ups. Especially when those mistakes got somebody killed.

The younger Charlie, now the boss, never screwed up, particularly when his decisions meant death. That was why he was in charge.

Weapons lockers stacked in the back, car stuffed with specialists on a mission to save the world—well, maybe a corner of it—Skosh drove toward the highway with Charlie next to him and three more killers sitting behind. The dark blue eyes of the youngest, Rimas, had aged a century in the two years since he had entered the world of black operations.

Jade led the way, meaning her passenger, Mack, led the way. Skosh tried not to let it bother him when she made every turn to the safehouses without a flaw, including a couple of double-right turns to dry-clean their route.

Mack is instructing her—because he knows where the house is, knows the route to it. Skosh's jaw tightened. The team knew every detail of his arrangements before he briefed them. Of course, they did. It was their superb grasp of detailed intelligence that allowed them to command big bucks when a government needed help with a delicate situation involving death. Besides money, their fees included information from everyone who hired them. They were a walking, seldom talking, often shooting team of operatives known as specialists.

And they had sent Skosh's predecessor, Frank, ahead—to assist him, they said. As a trusted retainer on the team's payroll, Frank would have told them all about the arrangements. The perfect situation: two houses in a worn-out residential neighborhood of short-term rentals that housed itinerant strangers intent upon their own business. Dream accommodation in an intelligence operation. And they were cheap.

Skosh worked for Uncle Sam, though the government would never admit it. His unofficial job title was babysitter, responsible for providing the support the team, known as Charlemagne, would need to accomplish what they had been hired to do. He technically didn't need the assistance of Jade, his section's librarian, but the team always requested her because, well, because Rimas. He ground his teeth at the thought.

FOUR

"We weren't expecting you," said Jade. She negotiated the airfield and turned left by order of Mack, who pointed the way using his whole hand, not just a finger. A long-ago childhood stricture against finger-pointing came to mind. "It's rude," her mother once told her. Of course, Mack would never do anything rude. The Austrian specialist might cut your throat but with faultless etiquette.

She glanced sideways, wondering if he would speak. So far, not. She tried another greeting.

"How have you been?"

More silence.

"How is Alex?"

She wondered how she managed to remember the name of the man's wife after seeing only a bare mention in a highly classified report encrypted on a caveated disk in a secure safe within her library vault. A woman she had never met and most likely never would meet. She found it difficult to imagine this guy in any domestic setting. Did he wear his gun to bed, she wondered? Did he use that knife to cut the tags off new clothes? Did he clean the blood off in the sink beforehand?

He spoke with a heavy accent. "Turn right. Do it now."

The tires squealed a bit despite the car's superb handling. This was an anti-surveillance maneuver, Jade knew. She had been studying tradecraft at Skosh's insistence. Skosh turned behind them. His move was less dramatic but every bit as hasty.

After a few more precautions, they reached a straight street and Mack relaxed.

"You have cut your hair," he said.

"Yes." A simple enough acknowledgment of the obvious, but Jade could not help a minor whine to go with it. "I got tired of trying to take care of it when Charlie made Skosh bring me along every time he hired you guys. The last place was a hell hole. There wasn't even a toilet—just a bucket behind a shed. I fail to see why you need a librarian in such places. I deal in electronic information. I cannot produce it where there is no electricity."

She tried glaring at him, taking in the expensive suit and silk tie, the blond and grey hair and very blue eyes staring back frankly with an amused half-smile.

"A remarkable progression from two years ago, Jade. Are you telling me you no longer believe it necessary to take a bath during an operation without a lock on the door?"

"There is no lock you guys can't defeat."

"What does Rimas think of your haircut?"

He had kept her in the car when Rimas came down the steps. The sedan's window tint would not reveal who was driving, let alone show her hairstyle. Rimas rode in the car behind, probably wondering where she was.

She answered Mack's question with silence, glanced right, and saw him smile again.

As Jade turned into the street leading to their two safehouses, she said, "Why are you even here? I thought you retired for good." Silently, she added *riddance.*

"I am here on an ancillary matter. It will have no bearing on Charlie's operation."

There was a note of uncertainty in that last bit and then a meaningful pause, so Jade filled it with what she knew was the team's mantra: "I know, I know, if you live."

"No, Jade, if *we* live. I include you."

She suppressed a shiver and signaled to turn at the next street to deposit Mack at the team's safehouse, but he waved her forward, indicating the narrow driveway at the side of a duplex Skosh and his old boss Frank had rented for themselves.

"That one's our house," she said. "For the babysitters."

Explanation unnecessary, she knew. The team made a point of both requiring and then cooperating on having their quarters separate from their handlers ever since she and Rimas had become an item two years ago. Awkward in the extreme, but better than occupying close quarters with that lot.

Jade stared ahead as the car came to a stop, remembering how this guy used language. "Why we? Are you saying I'm also in danger this time? I mean, more than usual?"

She expected his customary half-smiling silence, but as he opened his door, he said, "No. You must know your peril by now." The man knew how to make her shiver.

The two back-to-back safehouses shared a chain-link fence running through roughly mown scrub grass to a high brick wall along a street on one side and a lower wooden fence at the mid-point of the babysitters' building. They would stay in one half of a duplex, sharing a wall with an older man in the process of moving out. Skosh had arranged to pick up that lease as soon as the house was officially vacant. He would leave it empty as a buffer for additional security. The team's house faced a parallel street. Larger and more private, it included a garage with access directly into the house, handy for obscuring the comings and goings of a team of men in peak condition. Not that anyone in this hardscrabble environment would have time to notice. Invisibility was universally prized.

Rimas skirted the garage along the brick wall and smiled at Jade over the chain link as she locked the sedan. A hopeful smile, she thought with a sigh. He was sweet, kind, an excellent lover, and a journeyman assassin. She was stuck in a situation but, sadly, not stuck on him.

Skosh came around the same side of that house and told Rimas Charlie wanted him before climbing the fence to meet her at the back door. She stood, hand on the knob, leaning her forehead into the paneled wood. *Why* did Mack say *we*?

Mack stepped up and joined Skosh in looming over her. She was aware of the patience they practiced as they waited for her to gather her wits about her. She dealt with the jumble of emotions she held for each of them. Mingled fear, awe, and appreciation for Mack, the team's founder. Total, hopeless longing for Skosh, their babysitter. Why was Mack here? Because there weren't enough fucking complications in this situation. She caught herself thinking like Skosh. If she wasn't careful, she would soon be using the f-word out loud and just as creatively. The word already inhabited her interior thoughts, at least whenever they came out on an op with Charlemagne. She led the way into the kitchen.

"What the fuck are you doing, Frank?" Skosh stood red-faced inside the kitchen door, staring at a woman's tank top draped over a kitchen chair. It was not Jade's —she avoided pink, even in a narrow stripe around the hem. Frank sat at the table, his naturally tonsured head ruffled at the edges of the white hair circling a bald dome. Round, bulging eyes looked to the ceiling with exaggerated patience.

"Language, my boy, language. I told you about her. She's our link to them. They're looking for her. I'll explain it to Charlie if you don't want to."

"She?" Mack draped a suit bag over another chair next to the kitchen table.

Frank nodded. "A woman. A witness. Don't worry, there's room. This is a three-bedroom house. She and Jade can share, and so can Skosh and I. We'll show you where you'll bunk after Skosh detach... diseng... removes himself from off the ceiling."

"I can't let the team use a Canadian dangle, Frank,' said Skosh. "You fucking know that."

"She's American."

Mack interrupted. "Nationality is immaterial. She cannot stay here. *I* am staying here."

"She has to."

Skosh loosened his tie and unbuttoned the top button of his white shirt, glancing sideways at Mack. "You know Charlie will find a way to put her in jeopardy if she's here, Frank."

Frank pushed back his chair and looked up at Mack, then Skosh. His voice became soft, the words precisely chosen and rehearsed. "Either way, she's dead. Who knows? Charlie might be the only one who can keep her alive. Besides, that little dog is devoted to her. You wouldn't want him orphaned now, would you?"

Skosh held up a hand. "One thing at a time before we start talking about dogs." He turned to Mack. "What the fuck are you here for?"

"That is my business," came the usual still, even reply.

After two years, the man had not lost the ability to send a chill down Jade's spine. It was the stillness of his manner that called up the indelible memory of watching him kill three men with all due speed. Watching him move was worse. Sure it was. But every time he got that still, she remembered how quickly things could change.

Skosh leaned over the sink, elbows on the counter, one hand on his forehead. "You're a fucking piece of work, Frank. You know that? So why is she supposedly a dead woman walking, and, by the way, when were you going to tell me about Mack joining this shit show? The team's house is crammed already."

"It's not like your worrying could change it, Skosh. And Mack's staying with us, not in the team's house. Anyway, she's dead because she can identify Chatham. He killed a guy right in front of her in a park. Broad daylight."

"So?"

"So he knows. He can find her."

"How's that?"

"She described it on local TV news. The camera even lingered on the dog."

"A dog. Fuck." Skosh ran a hand through his mop of straight black hair.

Jade loved everything about the man, even his language, but especially the way his body moved as he stretched again to touch the low kitchen ceiling. The slow military flight to Vermont had been cramped; the beat-up rental car they used to cross the border seemed designed without shocks. He needed the stretch, she knew, and she enjoyed the watching.

But he lowered his arms abruptly when the dog barked.

FIVE

Christine Barton forgot to hush the dog as she walked into the kitchen because the older man's strange blue eyes held her fast. She had encountered enough criminals to recognize that dangerous stare. He watched; he assessed. She held firm, careful to hide her sinking stomach. In her long career, she had never before met this level of professionalism. Had the funny, round-eyed older man—what was his name—Frank? Had he brought her into a trap by promising protection?

Fool—I better leave.

Fluffy stopped barking, cowed by tension he could smell. She picked him up.

"Ah, Ms Barton," Frank said with a smile she was beginning to mistrust. She had found his concern for her safety touching, thought she might learn something here because she suspected he was a Fed, and agreed to his plan for her own reasons.

"Let me introduce John Nakamura and Jade Wilmerton." Turning to them, he said, "Miss Christine Barton and...?" He raised his brow in a question mark as he gestured at her smooth-haired brown and white rat terrier.

"Fluffy." Every eyebrow in the room rose, except, of course, for the criminal who wouldn't care. She added, "Because he's not."

The criminal required no introduction, but she needed an ID. She directed her words toward him.

"And you are?"

Judging by the shocked looks from, again, everybody but him, she knew they knew what he was.

Must be trap.

His smile was all the confirmation she needed.

"Um... call him Mack," said Frank.

She hugged Fluffy closer to her, remembered her responsibility for his protection, and decided to play innocent. He licked her chin.

"Very nice to meet you," she said to the criminal without smiling. He turned up a lip at one corner but said nothing. Turning to Frank, she said, "I appreciate your concern for me, Mr. Cardova, but I'm sure there is no more danger. If I can call my friend again, I'll find my way home to Vermont."

Mack, the criminal, spoke for the first time. "I am afraid you cannot, Miss Barton." He was foreign, with a heavy, probably German, accent.

Great. A Nazi criminal.

Had she told Frank her Abenaki middle name? She couldn't remember. Despite her training and experience, the events of the early morning sped by like a blurry movie on fast forward. The fractionally-white DNA in her ancestry provided background only. She could be mistaken for many mixtures but never white. Not a good thing, then, to be in the presence of a Nazi killer. She had seen one of those shoot a black man not two hours ago. Frank was looking increasingly untrustworthy for a Fed.

Before she could argue, Mack spoke again. "I assure you, you are in no danger from us. But if you fall into the hands of our—let us call them adversaries—you will become a danger to us."

Does he read minds?

"Let me guess, then *you'll* become a danger to *me*," she said, hugging her dog again. She kicked herself for abandoning the innocent ploy.

Big mouth. No cunning.

"Very good," said Mack. Despite the compliment, if he was impressed, he hid it well. He took a walking stick from the woman they called Jade standing behind him and leaned heavily on it.

Left hip. Wonderful. A wounded, foreign, probably Nazi, mind-reading criminal. Adversaries?

She contemplated running, but the door was locked behind that tall Asian man, the one named Nakamura. Even Jade looked like she could run way faster than Christine, especially considering her need to protect Fluffy. She would never abandon him. Before she could formulate a plan, running or not, a younger man came through the locked door, slipped what she knew to be a lock-picking tool into a pocket, and dropped a heavy, clanking duffel bag onto silver-flecked linoleum in front of a small—by American standards—refrigerator.

He spoke to the criminal in what she supposed was German.

Another Nazi. Great. Why so beautifully packaged? Nazis should be ugly, like their souls.

This one had hair almost as dark as hers and eyes a darker blue than the criminal's, with a thick white scar snaking from one of them toward his left temple. He stood tall and lanky like a gazelle, built for speed. Between him and Nakamura, there would be no hope of outrunning them if they gave chase. She abandoned the idea and caught herself wondering what it might be like to be caught by this one.

But then, if he's a Nazi, nothing good could come of it. And anyway, he's too young.

He smiled at Jade.

Ah, I see.

SIX

"Charlie wants to know if you will attend the meeting," Rimas said to Misha as he quickly scanned the room. "In five minutes."

Jade did not return his smile. Why? A strange woman with dark hair stood holding something that moved. Why, again? The babysitters must have fucked up, Rimas decided. They have allowed a Canadian woman into their safehouse. Surely, they knew Misha was coming. Frank was present during the planning. Rimas settled his eyes on the woman's face. Not young, but hard to tell the age, with high cheekbones, full lips, concerned eyes, and... a dog?

Skosh and Frank have really fucked up.

Misha answered him, but he was too busy making conjectures to hear it. Before he could find a way to hide the lapse, the older man snapped. "Tell him to expect me."

Rimas took another look at the Canadian woman and turned to leave, wondering how Misha would eliminate this new threat.

Pity. She is rather pretty.

. . .

When Misha joined him outside, Rimas held the cane as he hopped the fence adroitly, the only clue to the injury passing in a momentary wince as he landed. He didn't think Rimas had seen it.

"She may be dirty," said Misha as he took back his cane.

"Who? The woman you told me about? The one Vasily liked here in Montreal so many years ago?"

"No." Misha used his stick to point backward to the babysitters' house. "That one. With the dog."

"How do you know?"

"I do not know. I only suspect. She recognized me and sees me as an enemy."

"She knows who you are?"

Misha sighed. Patience was not his predominant quality at the best of times, but he forced himself to seek it. Rimas had more than just skill. He had talent. With the right guidance, Rimas would someday become a formidable operative. If he listened to Misha. And if he lived.

"She does not know who I am. She knows what I am," he explained.

"Was it like that with Vasily's girl, Gloria?"

"Not entirely the same, but close."

Rimas paused a few feet short of the door to the team's safehouse, raising his brow in a question mark that gratified Misha. He was listening, developing a searching insistence on complete information, taking care to understand and trace connections behind everything he learned. It made Rimas a good fit in the field of intelligence despite his perilous habit of discounting the unpredictability of emotion.

So Misha took a moment to stop and explain more thoroughly than usual. "When Gloria met me, I saw a glimpse, a shadow of caution in her eyes. She was careful to limit eye contact, to keep her hands empty and always visible to me."

"And Vasily?"

"That was more important. He was more dangerous than me. I thought this should be plain to most people because of his solemn, closed and wary manner. He had very light grey eyes that saw all people as threats. He issued a challenge with every stare." Misha moved into the shadow under the wall to his right and watched Rimas clear the fence with effortless grace. "Gloria's behavior around Vasily was too playful, too fond," he continued. "Someone who could react to me, quickly hide it, and then pretend not to know about him must be dirty. I warned Vasily."

"Did he listen?"

"Of course not. He considered all American women exotic. This was a blonde who wore a miniskirt. He became infatuated, entranced. Much like you are with Jade."

Rimas narrowed his eyes and blurted, "Jade has dark hair. Nothing similar."

"She is American."

"But not dirty. You said so."

"No. Not dirty," agreed Misha."

Rimas blew a sigh of relief, glanced back at the safehouse where Jade was staying, and said more slowly, "But this other woman, the Canadian?"

"Also American, not Canadian. She not only recognized me, she challenged me with her stare. She has had training and is not afraid."

"Jade was not afraid when she met you."

"Not sufficiently, that is true. She did not understand. This one does, like Gloria."

"Then how is she different from Gloria?"

"She does not pretend. And I wonder what is the purpose of the dog?" He paused. "I can see more questions in your eyes. Ask."

Rimas inhaled sharply, breathed out, and said, "I wondered how Vasily could be more dangerous than you, but then there is also Michael, after all."

Misha gave an almost smile to the young fighter who was blithely unaware of his own lethality. He held open the door to the garage. Rimas followed him in, still wondering about that dog.

SEVEN

M ichael stood to preside over the meeting, feeling both his authority and its burden of responsibility. His team assembled with coffee in the living room, a long, narrow space with an open kitchen at one end, where the all-important coffee maker dominated a short counter along the back wall. A kitchen island created an aisle before it. The lumpy sofa of an indeterminate color closely resembling dirt provided a place to sit along a staircase wall, but nobody chose it. Stiff-backed wooden dining chairs filled that need and were preferred by everyone except him.

The others no doubt wondered, but Michael knew why his father had joined them on this op. What he didn't fathom was how he felt about it. He was smug in the knowledge his wife, Theresa, would never dictate his movements. *Only because she's too busy* came the immediate mental correction to the thought. She trusted him absolutely to do his job, never interfering in team matters like this. She had learned that lesson the hard way several years ago. Why was Alex so insistent with his father?

He opened the meeting, saying, "Chatham arrived in Montreal fifteen hours ago and evaded most of our watchers within an hour. We'll get Skosh in here in a few minutes so he can tell us what he learned from the Canadians. In the meantime, let's go over the bare bones of what we know. Steve?"

Steve tore his eyes from an unframed daguerreotype hanging askew on the wall beside him, showing Sherlock Holmes falling from a cliff, the evil Moriarty chortling at the top. He took a slow sip of his coffee and cleared his throat. "Chatham's a good old Southern boy, a proud patriot, saved Christian, and fucking effective killer. His favorite targets are blacks and liberals. We don't know who he works for, but we've suspected, and now we know for sure he's not free-lance because he's too emotional. He goes off the rails sometimes, and somebody else has to come along and clean it up."

"How do we know this for sure?" Sergei walked to the machine for a refill, savored a sip, and waited for the reply. His worried, almost colorless eyes gazed at the liquid in his cup until he drained it and poured again. Michael noticed the distracted behavior. The man's mind was elsewhere.

"Before they lost him today," said Steve, "one of our watchers, not Skosh's, heard a shot and saw him run out of the park through a narrow screen of trees on one side. He stopped in a cafe on another street."

Sergei handed him the half-empty mug in his hand, turned to the coffee machine again, and poured into a clean cup. Steve stared at the two cups he now held, put them down on the counter, and pulled a crumpled sheet of notebook paper out of a pocket.

"Chatham's on the lam after a killing," he said, "and he stops for coffee and to write a fucking letter. He's pissed off and careless. Not even using code. The watcher followed him to the drop he used but lost him in an alley. So he went for the letter and brought it to Skosh."

"They put it back after I copied it," said Michael. "I don't think Chatham's people are alerted. It took less than half an hour, but the empty drop had only one watcher on it for that length of time."

"Is that the paper Skosh gave you at the airplane? Why have I not seen it?" Sergei gulped more coffee while standing at the machine, still not sitting down.

Michael could see he wasn't handling stress well and would be pinging with coffee jitters for hours. "You were on the satellite phone with Mara. I couldn't get your attention."

"She had two contractions," said Sergei, his Russian accent more pronounced than usual, eyes on the phone. "Far apart, she said."

"My sister can handle contractions, Sergei. Your daughter is proof of that."

"But this is a son! I worry."

Michael was about to tell his brother-in-law that baby boys are no more dangerous than girls, but he looked at Steve and Rimas and the twitch in Sergei's eye and wished Mara were on this op, not facing death during the ordinary practice of giving life. He wanted it because she was the most sane member of the team. Apart from himself. Maybe.

Steve continued. "The language Chatham used in his letter before going to ground was like you'd say to your boss, 'I fucked up, please don't punish me for it.' We doubled the watchers on both the drop and its approaches. They're deep and round the clock, waiting for whoever services it. We might get a line on who that boss is if we can hold on to the trail of a courier."

Michael ignored the deferential glance Steve sent his way when describing mistakes confessed to a boss. He liked to think he did not make a habit of painful corrections. The consequences of anybody's errors were usually punishment enough—for all of them. What worried him more was the absence of a similar glance from Sergei, who was the one most likely to fuck things up this time around.

Rimas set his empty mug next to the computer by his chair under another waterfall picture—one of several in this room, but this one did not feature Holmes. He stood and said, "Shall I go get Skosh now?"

Michael briefly wondered if having just one Watson when an obedient bit of muscle might come in handy would be easier than this. He loved these guys and depended on them, but had to resist the urge to bury his face in his hands when their minds were so scattered. Instead, he looked pointedly at the secure radio beside him and shifted the stare to Rimas, willing him to read his eyes.

You will not, I repeat not, spend your time looking for Jade.

Rimas blanched. At least he caught on quickly.

Michael's father cleared his throat and waited for a nod before speaking as if he meant to stay out of this op.

"There is another more recent development. Perhaps you should inform us." Misha addressed Rimas, who wrinkled his brow.

"Do you mean the woman?"

Steve groaned softly, "Not another one."

"Go on," said Michael.

"She is Canadian—no, American—pretty, with very dark hair like Jade, and she is staying in Jade's room. Also, she has a dog, and Misha thinks she is dirty."

"She saw Chatham kill the man in the park," said Misha, "and told police, the press, the world. Frank has rescued her." He explained the behaviors that made him suspicious, sparking a five-minute team argument about why an older woman evidently trained to recognize a fighter would have the confidence to challenge him.

Steve once again made himself indispensable by coming up with the solution in his slow Texas drawl, brown eyes languid under long lashes.

"She's a cop."

EIGHT

S kosh suppressed a momentary annoyance at the summons from Charlie. It wasn't the fact of the call or the nature of the meeting he was told to attend. These were routine. It was the respectful treatment he was getting from these fucking killers. Okay, he had to admit it. He had killed during that op on the Curonian Spit two years before. He had no choice. He didn't tell any of his government colleagues in The Section and didn't put it in the report because, well, that would have been the end of his career working for Uncle Sam. Babysitters don't kill. Period. But Sergei had seen it, and the team kept no secrets from each other.

He dragged his feet as he crossed the shaded pair of yards and jumped the fence to the other house, the one with different occupants, damn it. Different. He was not one of them. He would never be one of them.

At least the team had been decent enough to keep quiet about it.

"Took you long enough." Sergei held the door to the garage open for him. Again, the respectful gesture mixed with disdainful words.

Skosh received the jibe with the coldly impassive glance he had been practicing. To his mind, anybody who thought Asians came naturally to inscrutability must be racist. Typically, his emotions wrote themselves all over his face and trumpeted f-words from his mouth. Sergei had seen him break a guy's neck. The memory helped Skosh maintain the muscles of his face. Distance, maintain distance, he reminded himself. *Breathe*.

This house was different, more open, with no kitchen, per se, only a continuation of the living room. The coffee machine was the same, of course, and the old prints on the walls. Circa way back, all of them pictures of waterfalls, and every one crooked.

"Skosh," said Charlie as he entered from the side door under the stairs, "my father tells us you have a house guest. I must meet her."

With any luck, only the coffee machine witnessed his grimace; he was headed straight toward it. He controlled the tension in his back, poured, and turned, mug in hand. He gave a minimal nod.

"But only me," added Charlie. "She has already seen my father. I don't want her to see the rest of the team."

"She has seen Rimas," said Mack, holding out his mug to Skosh.

"And Rimas," agreed Skosh. He brought the pot and poured flawlessly into the suspended cup. No splashes. Meditation was beginning to work. He rooted himself to the earth beneath the house and felt every muscle become simultaneously relaxed and ready. Even the steady stare he exchanged with Mack's quelling blue eyes did not shake it.

Mack smiled.

Is that how these guys do it?

Goat Rope

Skosh was pleased with his progress but not interested in becoming any more like them. He took a deep pull at his mug before changing the subject.

"We're trying to find out who is in town and who might be the guy Chatham wrote that letter to. Frank has a few older contacts among the Canadians. Retired colleagues. He's getting background on the more violent right-wing groups in Quebec and specifically asked for names of old members of the FLQ who are still around. They were Marxists, but he says that doesn't matter."

Mack nodded. "Frank was with us here in 1971 after the October Crisis. Do not expect ideological consistency from zealots. They are easily manipulated into violence. The KGB was always very good at that. Racist propaganda is as effective a tool as class division in keeping the West busy with internal threats."

"FLQ?" asked Rimas, eyebrows high with surprise. "Was that when Vasily met Gloria? What crisis?"

Mack nodded. "The FLQ were French nationalists, mostly bombers and bank robbers, but in October 1970, they took hostages, a British diplomat and a Canadian minister. The diplomat lived. The minister did not. We arrived in January to take care of the American involvement. Frank was our babysitter."

Skosh stepped away from the coffee machine and headed for an uncomfortable chair under a torn poster of a black cat, the only non-waterfall in the room. The caption was in French. He remembered a time when he didn't speak any European languages and longed for sushi on the Ginza. Steve hit him in the stomach with an empty mug as he passed. It was an overly familiar way to ask for a refill. He would have preferred the usual sneering demand.

I'm not one of you.

He wanted to shout it, but he refilled both cups instead.

"I've read your file all the way back to the '60s," he said to Mack as he handed Steve his cup. "There is no mention of an op in Montreal."

Silence and deleted official information. The team had infiltrated the system, as usual. It must have been done decades before when his latest safeguards were not in place. Rimas's question meant the old Montreal op involved the late Sobieski, explosives expert and martial artist on the original team, who was killed in the early '80s. Had Mack suddenly become the grizzled old uncle telling the younger generation fun stories of youthful exploits? Skosh looked at him sitting there, still as a stone, not a greyish-blond hair out of place, in a pricey suit and Italian shoes. Nothing grizzled about him, he decided. Mack caught his eye and smiled.

Yep. Still reading minds.

"At least, it would be nice to know what the American involvement was," he said between sips. He stood next to the machine, now reluctant to sit down anywhere. Unwilling to get comfortable. Determined to maintain his newfound control.

Mack glanced toward Charlie before answering with a shrug. "There was cooperation between the FLQ and a nationalist group in the US. The American group sent a specialist to exact revenge upon two targets. One was a Canadian press official the FLQ blamed for their almost immediate loss of public support. The other provided information that put most of them in prison or exile within the next ten years. They succeeded against the press official before we got here."

"Are there parallels?" asked Charlie.

"Yes."

"Metaphorical or direct?"

"Both, I suppose, but mostly direct."

Now Mack had everybody's attention. He looked to the ceiling, into the past, before answering. "First, the cooperation between foreign nationalist groups has not changed. Second, for us, it was a simple commission to stop an American specialist and his network from assassinating a Canadian official. That is all. The moment we landed, it became more complex. The official was already dead, and we learned our target had an accomplice. Then, the danger to the informant came to Frank's attention. Almost too late."

Skosh had become involved in the conversation, realizing Mack would not waste words on any immaterial part of the story. He could not keep from tilting his head as he asked, "I get the nationalism, and now that our guy has written a love letter to his boss, it can only mean he's got an accomplice here. I get that, too, but what else? It was twenty-eight years ago. Things are different."

"They are not."

The smile was either approving or condescending. Vintage Mack.

The secure phone next to the computer rang, and Sergei answered it as Steve said, "How so?"

Again, Mack took his time. At that moment, lightning struck and Skosh knew the answer. "Because of the woman Frank has picked up," he said.

Mack smiled his approval. "It remains to be seen whether she is the endangered informant or a deadly accomplice." He looked at his son. "I recommend you use her until she makes a mistake.

NINE

C hristine studied the young man sitting across from her at the small kitchen table in what she had heard Frank call a safehouse. She did not feel safe. Did the man even blink? Not so as to be noticed. He was that motionless. Blond, impeccably and expensively dressed, like the older Nazi with a cane, but this one had no accent. Still, he felt foreign.

Frank sat to her right and made introductions.

"This is Charlie," he said, indicating the blond glacier. "And you met Rimas earlier."

Christine glanced to her left. "I saw him; I didn't meet him." She made a habit of correcting the record.

She returned Charlie's cold belligerence, knowing she was outclassed here and, more importantly, outnumbered. Frank had seemed okay. A government type, oozing bureaucratic authority. These two, Charlie and Rimas, would be best described as perps.

At long last, Charlie broke the subject, though not the stare.

"Ms. Barton, your description of the man you saw was remarkably thorough. We wonder who taught you to be so observant."

Definitely foreign.

He tilted his head and raised one eyebrow when she did not answer for several beats.

"I'm a State Trooper over the border in Vermont. I know how to describe a suspect. I also know when I'm looking at a criminal."

On her left, Rimas guffawed. Charlie threw him a warning glance and smiled. "And what is it that makes you *know* I am a criminal, Ms. Barton, or should I say, Officer Barton?"

"Lieutenant will do."

She reminded herself this was supposed to look like a holiday she gave herself as a reward for the long scramble and boatload of work it took to get the promotion.

So act like it.

She maintained steady contact with those ice-blue eyes as she answered.

"You move like a fighter. You're packing. You didn't introduce yourself as a government official. You're wary and alert. This is common to three of you: Rimas here and the guy with the cane. You, particularly, remind me of a large cat. That Asian guy..." She looked up at the man leaning against the counter behind Frank, sipping coffee from an enormous mug.

"Call me Skosh," he said. "You're not exactly white, either, so don't let me hear you call me 'Asian guy' again."

"I'm native. Abenaki on most of both sides. Sorry if I offended."

Touchy. He's got something going on.

She looked back at Charlie. "Skosh could also be government, but Frank here is not the kindly uncle-type I mistook him for."

"I'm only looking out for your safety, my dear," said Frank.

"So you bring me to a den of thieves?"

"They're not thieves," said Skosh. "They give good value for their work. They're killers, assassins, expensive ones. Get your criminal categories straight, Lieutenant."

Frank sighed. "The proper term is specialist. They are intelligence operatives who specialize. And you are correct, Lieutenant, Skosh works for the federal government."

"Call me Christine. Can I see an ID?"

"No," said Skosh. "I don't carry one."

Charlie finally broke his impersonation of a statue and spoke. "Do you have a weapon with you?"

"Hell, no." Christine laid her hands flat on the table for emphasis. "I'm not going to try crossing a border with a firearm, am I? This is supposed to be a pleasure trip with a couple of friends. They're going to be worried."

Nicely skirted.

Frank hurried to assure her, "I left word for you at your hotel when I couldn't find them."

What a chum, but awkward. She decided against pressing it.

"Where is the dog?" asked Charlie.

Here was her Achilles heel, and he put his finger right on it. Fluffy was non-negotiable. He had been with her five years now, ever since she pulled duty at the holding facility and had to take the dogs on death row to the vet for imposition of sentence. Crime: being homeless, unloved, and a public health hazard. She identified, especially with the small, brown and white one. He looked at her and she knew. He wasn't all that young, like her. He'd had some bad breaks like her. One of those breaks left his right front leg inoperable. She took him home. Her vet removed the leg.

She took a deep breath. "He's curled up next to Jade on the bed. They're both asleep."

Will he threaten Fluffy?

"The dog is in no more danger than you are," said Charlie, "but he is distinctive and known to the man we are looking for. We will use it to find him."

"I'm not letting you take him. He only listens to me. Sorry, no can do."

Charlie leaned back and pointed to the coffee machine behind Skosh. Like an expensive coffee boy, Skosh poured another mug and handed it to him. She was not offered any.

Bastards.

"I will not take him," said Charlie. "You will. You will walk him in the same park several times a day. Your boyfriend here, Rimas, will walk with you and hold your hand. Maybe you'll kiss a little. You won't stay long, and you will leave in the same direction each time you walk your dog—at the same times each day."

"You think anybody will buy that? They'll think I'm his mother."

"No. They won't. They won't get that close."

"And if I say no?"

Charlie calmly sipped his coffee, saying nothing, never taking his eyes from her face.

"At least tell me if I'm aiding and abetting a bunch of Nazis," she said.

"You're not," answered Frank. "You're helping us hunt them."

TEN

"We've been down this street twice already," said Christine. "Why? Are we on patrol or something?"

Rimas grimaced. This woman was in the way. Not in the way of the op. Michael would take care of that. Her presence interfered with something more substantial—his ability to be alone with Jade. Steve's expression would be 'pain in the ass.'

"We're dry-cleaning our route," said Skosh from the front passenger seat.

Misha explained it more graciously as he turned the wheel for another right turn. "I am making it difficult for someone to follow us."

How could he be gracious to somebody he thought might be dirty, wondered Rimas.

Typical Misha understatement. He made it not difficult but impossible to tail the sedan. Without any sign of hurry, without squealing on the turns, Misha made it look easy. Michael could do that, to be sure, every bit as effectively, but you always knew he was concentrating. Misha acted like it was a summer outing to the park. Which it was, so to speak.

"Misha, if this woman is dirty, who will dispose of her?" Rimas used German. He doubted she knew the language, and if she did, the knowledge would not help her, only provide additional evidence of guilt. She blushed easily. If she understood, they would read it on her face.

Misha answered in English. "It is impolite to speak a language unknown to a person in the party."

"Nonetheless," continued Rimas in German, "who had to kill the one in 1971? You never finished the story."

"You try my patience," came Misha's reply in German. Switching to English, he said, "You should explain to Christine how she is to follow you out of the car when we stop. It may be difficult for her with the dog."

Explain? Rimas looked at the woman. The dog panted in her lap, his large ears pointing up, alert. "Quickly," he said, then thought for a moment and added, "Very quickly."

Skosh turned in his seat to look at them both. "Let me expand that for you just a little, Christine. Rimas will pull you out of the car when we're slow but not quite stopped. Just keep Fluffy in your arms and go with the flow. He'll have an arm around you so you don't fall over. Right, Rimas?"

"When...?" She could not finish the question. The car slowed, and Rimas opened the door. He grabbed her arm none too gently. The dog growled at him, but she held Fluffy securely as they melted into the crowded sidewalk, Rimas's hand tight around her waist.

"All right, all right!" she said. "Let go so I can walk."

She stepped on his instep, and he glared at her.

"Not my fault," she insisted. "Let me walk."

He loosened his grip enough to stop interfering with each step but not enough to give her the impression she could make a run for it.

"Why did it have to be you?" she asked. "Why is Charlie making me do this at all, let alone with an arrogant son-of-a-bitch like you?"

"Be quiet!" He used a harsh whisper, leaning into her ear as if to kiss her neck. "Too many people."

"An arrogant man of many words, I see."

He furrowed his brow.

"Sarcasm," she said.

Steve used a phrase with that word. What was it? Rimas remembered and decided it would not betray anything if overheard.

"It does not become you." He tossed the words at her.

Her unsuppressed laugh made him smile, not because it helped their cover as a pair of lovers out for a stroll, though it did. The sound of it sent a shiver of delight. Her low, dusky, rolling laughter made her even prettier, he decided.

"Now what?" she asked as they entered the park. Their feet crunched over a gravel path, staying clear of bushes and open to view on all four sides of the little green rectangular space. Rimas felt exposed. He reminded himself the team had his back and forced the muscles in his neck to relax.

"Now we walk slowly," he said, "and we talk."

"About what?"

He shrugged. "Anything. Just make it look good. What are you doing?" He looked down at her, appalled.

She had pulled a small plastic bag from her pocket and stooped over the grass where the dog had done its business. She put the bag over it and picked it up!

"Don't look at me like that," she said. "It's only polite to pick up after your dog before somebody steps in it."

"Misha tries to make me polite, but he never mentioned picking up shit."

"Misha?"

"Mack. You must call him Mack. Nothing else."

"I mentally called him the criminal Nazi until the government guy told me he's not. A Nazi, I mean. Not sure about the criminal part. So are you one of them or another fed?"

"Fed?" He stopped and looked down at her. Traffic drove by them a few yards to his left. With any luck, word would get to the target soon, and he could spend a little time with Jade.

"Federal officer. Do you work for Uncle Sam or Mack, the possible criminal?"

He struggled with 'work for.' Michael was the boss, certainly, but that was by unanimous consent because Michael's judgment never failed. How to explain? Must he explain? If she was dirty, she deserved no explanation. He looked down at her full lips bent in a half smile, her good humor sparkling from brown eyes. There were worse assignments. He tilted her chin and bent to kiss her. It was part of the job, after all.

"Well?" Her voice came quieter as they continued their slow walk, with Fluffy sniffing every blade of grass along the way. She still wanted an answer.

"I am a member of the team. It is not employment. It is membership."

"What team?"

"Charlemagne. The team is called Charlemagne."

"You're one of them? The guys Skosh told me about? You're an assassin?"

Was it the question or the kiss that made this conversation uncomfortable? He did not want to answer it. At the same time, he knew the quality of his next kiss depended on truth.

"Yes."

ELEVEN

Jade drew the short straw on this op. Nothing was as usual. Nobody behaved normally. Then again, they never did, did they? But this was abnormally abnormal. Well, maybe Rimas still threw her a few longing looks, but why was Mack acting like a babysitter? They had swapped cars, and he was driving.

"I should drive," she insisted. "I know how to evade surveillance now."

Mack glanced at her, then at the mirror, and made a sharp left across Montreal traffic so smoothly nobody even honked.

"I know," he said. "You study tradecraft. Are you dissatisfied with your library?"

"No."

"Your job, then? Is that why you practice what you are learning? Are you trying to become a babysitter?"

"No, are you? I thought you retired."

"I did. I am retired. I do not mind an occasional support role. Are you disappointed in Skosh?"

He pressed again when she did not answer.

"In Rimas?"

Jade contemplated her answer. She wanted finesse, truth, and tact sufficient not to irritate the man next to her. She could not tell what he was thinking and knew his mind-reading fame was no exaggeration. Neither was his reputation as a killer. She had seen both—multiple times.

For that matter, she had also seen Rimas kill. And Skosh, though that was never mentioned. Killing was not in the babysitter job description. Though he had not been at fault, Jade sensed his deep dismay when it happened two years ago. But each time she saw Rimas, he became more like the man next to her—much too much used to it. Were their nightmares like hers, or worse? Worse, she decided.

"Um." She cleared her throat. "I enjoy his company." She turned her head to watch the side mirror on her right, hoping he would not see the blush.

"You enjoy the sex. Do you love him?"

"You don't beat around the bush, do you? Do you like asking questions you already know the answer to?"

Was that a smile or a grimace? She hoped for a smile. Not good to irritate this man, retired or not.

The radio squawked. Charlie told everybody to begin leading their possible tails in different directions. Christine and Rimas had been picked up by Skosh and Frank near the park and were on their way north.

Mack turned right, then right again before saying, "I require you to speak it so that the sound remains in your ears. Do you love him?"

She sighed and closed her eyes. "No. I like him. But love? No." Her words rang in her heart. Would

Mack try to convince her she was wrong? Hadn't she already tried to persuade herself a million times?

"Then you must tell him."

She choked at the impossibility. "How?"

This time, there was a smile. "I believe there are many popular songs with advice on this topic. Pick one."

"But I.... he's so emotional, infatuated..." She swallowed the next word, *deadly.*

Mack supplied it, "A fighter. But he is not a madman. One does not have to be a specialist to react badly to such news. The reverse is also true. Many people suffer similar disappointments without resorting to violence, even specialists." Mack took a deep breath and let it out in a huff. "Words I have heard repeatedly from my wife."

"Alex?"

He nodded.

"She's breaking up with you?"

He snorted and took one hand off the wheel to point with his whole hand forward into an imaginary list of arguments he had been required to memorize.

"No. She cannot. She assures me she has no desire to, but also reminds me that once you move to Vasily's Carpet, there is no safe exit. Our enemies..."

"Vasily's Carpet?"

"Where. We. Live."

She got the impression this would be the only explanation but could not help goading him just a little.

"You live in a carpet? Like fleas?"

He clenched his jaw and took a deep breath.

"My point is, if you do not love him, you cannot successfully live at Vasily's Carpet."

"Define successful."

He glared at her, checked his mirrors, and took another turn.

"I don't have the heart to hurt him," she said softly. "He is easily hurt, you know."

"I do. He is much like Vasily in that respect, though not as damaged."

"Vasily?"

"My friend from childhood. A founder of the team. He was killed many years ago." He paused as he sped through an amber light, eyes on the rearview. "It was Vasily who first called me Misha. He was very solemn, even as a child. He grew up in my house because his parents were killed when he was four years old. His mother died at the hands of the KGB, but we believe it was she who shot his father. He never spoke much and had little that could be called conversation in any language, but was a mathematical genius. Also, he was a deadly fighter."

"Charming. Is that the damage you mentioned, the loss of his parents?"

"Partly. It is where Rimas and he differ because Rimas had conscientious parents. He grew up more normally. Vasily's difficulty with talking was a problem, especially with women. It was not helped when the woman who made love to him for the first time tried to kill him. He killed her instead."

Appalling. She suppressed it. He was continuing, and it felt unwise to interrupt. Mack was not exactly a chatterbox. This conversation had a purpose that involved her. Alex must be a powerful woman.

Mack continued. "He was very young when he became active. Vasily's uncles in Poland encouraged him, and he took up the fight against the communists before age fifteen. His first kill occurred shortly after. He was captured often and tortured equally often. When he was eighteen, Louis and I helped him escape. Once he was free, he shot the woman who betrayed him. That was our first op—when we became Charlemagne."

Jade maintained as matter-of-fact a tone as she could manage. "You're saying Vasily killed before he had sex? And if I may ask, who is Louis?"

"Louis was also our friend and grew up in my house because his uncle Bertrand was training him to fight. Bertrand trained all of us. Louis was killed early in this decade in a place called San Antonio."

"I've heard of it." Jade reeled under the concept of children being trained to fight but kept her eyes on the street ahead.

"When your enemies are implacable," Mack said— just like him to read her mind—"you learn to fight or you die. This is why Alex insists if you do not love Rimas, you should not acquire our enemies. He was much older than Vasily was when he first killed a man, but in only two years, he has become noticeable to those who want us dead."

Time for another quick self-exam. *Do I love him? No. Care about him? Yes, a lot. But that's not a substitute. And who am I to think I am the only person he needs? Maybe if I free him, it will free me. Skosh ...*

As if the thought conjured it, Skosh's voice came over the radio. "Not pulling in with the package. Somebody is walking into the other half of the babysitter duplex. Doesn't look like the older man on the lease. Dry-cleaning our way to the team's quarters around the block."

Jade could not tell if the shiver running up her spine was the result of the bad news from the radio or the ultra-controlled anger in the voice next to her.

"What old man?" demanded Mack.

TWELVE

They were dancing a caffeine boogaloo. Christine saw Skosh bring a mug of the stuff to Charlie, where he sat in a corner easy chair, surveying the room, his eyes sometimes pausing on her with a scowl. She watched him from a straight-backed dining chair with her back to the window, across the room from the almighty coffee machine on the kitchen counter. They had all been out on this walk-the-dog adventure. If they learned anything, she sure didn't know it, nor have any idea what they were up to besides no good.

She abandoned all efforts at comprehending and concentrated instead on observing and mentally recording what she saw. It helped against the nagging worry, the overarching need for a telephone. The house was similar to the one they left, though larger, with a dark brick exterior and sash windows. The interior of this one had suffered a bad remodeling job in the recent past. The wall between the kitchen and living room had been removed, making one large room downstairs. Appliances were clustered at one end. A dirty, grey industrial carpet covered the floor throughout. To her left was a bolted front door, and behind her, a heavily curtained window.

Jade took a chair near the front door, next to a stack of footlockers barricading the door, partly blocking the landing of the staircase leading to the bedrooms upstairs. The big SUV had been squeezed into the narrow attached garage, and the Mercedes sedan was backed in on the drive in front of the garage door. The only door anybody used to enter the house was the one from the garage that opened under the staircase. To the right of the entrance, tucked in under the stairs, a doorway led down to a basement. Mack lay stretched out, coatless, on a shabby sofa shoved against the wall, feet toward the front door and the landing, left arm covering his eyes. A fully inhabited black leather shoulder holster gleamed against his white shirt.

At the other end of the long, narrow room, Skosh made more coffee. Charlie scanned a thick stack of connected tractor-feed paper fresh off a busy printer on a wobbly dining table against the long wall to Christine's right. A jumbled assortment of computer parts filled the rest of the table, with two monitors running stock screen savers in never-ending patterns of scrolls and swirls.

Frank dozed in another easy chair next to the table, his eyes bulging even behind closed lids. Funny old man, she thought. More like a bureaucrat than one of the criminals. Retired or not, still a Fed, like Skosh. She contemplated the words he had used when he pulled her from her hotel room.

"You're way too public a witness."

"I couldn't help it. The reporter met me coming out of the police station. He already had the camera running."

"It was not a simple murder. You need to come with me."

"Looked pretty simple to me. The guy shot a man right in front of me."

"You're in more danger than you know."

He won the argument, and here she was, feeling even more jeopardy, wishing she could use the telephone again. There was one on the wall by the computer.

Rimas sat in a third stiff chair against the long wall with a low coffee table before him under a crooked picture of a waterfall. There were several of these decorating the room, randomly breaking up otherwise blank white walls. He reassembled and reholstered his handgun, then pulled a rifle from the open footlocker next to him. Maybe that, too, was a semi-auto masquerading as something more to look cool, but she doubted it. There was nothing cool here—all strictly business.

How is this safer?

As if in response to her thought, two strange men walked in through the door under the stairs. The bulges under their arms, the bulges of their arms, the way they moved, the way they scanned the room, the way their eyes stopped for a long time on her face, her hands, and the dog in her lap, gave her the answer.

It's not.

...

Skosh had been standing next to Charlie under old Sherlock in free fall on the wall when he noticed him eyeing Christine. He could see the calculations speeding by behind those still, blue eyes. Charlie reached a decision a nano-second later, picked up his radio, and called the delinquents in from the car.

51

"Then you must not think she's dirty, Charlie," said Skosh, using German.

"I'm reserving judgment."

"Your father thinks she is."

"My father is living in the past. Steve and Sergei need sleep right now. They'll have to risk being seen. If she turns out dirty, they know what to do."

As if being mentioned in quiet conversation was enough to wake him, Mack pushed himself upright from his nap on the couch and limped toward them just as the delinquents came through the door. He studied the lieutenant sitting against the far wall before turning to scowl at Skosh.

"What old man has moved into your house?" he demanded.

Charlie raised an eyebrow to second the demand for a too-long delayed explanation.

Skosh sighed. He had been hoping for a chance at the coffee pot. "I couldn't get a lease for all three houses until next week, but I took the two empty ones and investigated the old man who still held that third lease. Very old. He checked out clear. My Canadian counterpart, Yannick, did the background check, and we have pictures. He's getting ready to move. We have surveillance. He's buying boxes. I saw the receipts. I put the babysitters' safehouse next to him in the duplex. It should have been okay—until this younger guy showed up."

"A relative?" suggested Steve as he and Sergei joined them.

Skosh shrugged.

Sergei scowled at him. "You said we would be able to secure our perimeters for both houses. We cannot monitor your house with a wall shared by an un-known. This is unsecure. They can put touches inside that wall. If this man finds the sensors I have in-stalled...."

Frank interrupted, handing out mugs of coffee to Steve and Sergei. "I verified the man's bona fides through our sources. There shouldn't be an unknown in that house. His closest kin lives in Vancouver. This new guy has New York plates."

"It's worse than just New York plates," said Skosh, wishing fervently for coffee. "He's in the game. He moved wrong. Too aware. And he's packing. His coat flapped open when he slung a backpack on one shoul-der. I saw a strap. It could only be a holster. He crossed the Canadian border with a firearm. He might not be a player in our game, but he's on somebody's team."

During the pause, all eyes on him, Skosh noticed Frank slip—more like slink—back to the coffee ma-chine. Four killers stared at Skosh with respect. Only coffee would alleviate this discomfort. But when even Frank, his old boss and fellow babysitter, gave him the same respectful look while serving him a steaming mug of the stuff, discomfort became despair.

"We must remove our sensors near that house," insisted Sergei, the team's gadget man. Skosh noticed he already needed a shave.

Steve took a long sip and nodded. His face was displaying a healthy crop of dark brown stubble. Skosh unconsciously felt his chin. Not as bad, he decided.

"And why not put touches in that wall?" suggested Steve.

Mack tapped the floor beneath his stick. "Another coincidence makes me uneasy. When we came here in

1971, there were also too many connections. We had only a narrow escape from disaster."

Charlie answered with a slight nod. "But sometimes coincidence can help us, Papa. You have always used what fate throws our way. I will do the same. The policewoman and her dog are in play for our purposes, and I think it's time to employ Skosh's unexpected talent."

Sputtering on his hot coffee, Skosh turned red. "Hold on. I'm a babysitter. I'm not …"

"Nobody said you were anything else. But you'll help tonight as usual."

"Not as usual. There is somebody in that house. If he's dirty and if there is a problem, it will require a specialist. This is more delicate."

"And you are more capable. Steve will lead. Sergei will stay back. Rimas can place touches. Skosh, you clear the sensors. Any questions?

"I shouldn't get that close to this," said Skosh. He looked down into the brown liquid cooling in his cup."

Charlie's answer came smoothly modulated.

"I said questions, not wishes."

THIRTEEN

"Can I help here? I'm bored to tears. Did you have a good nap?"

Rimas looked up at her, puzzled. Christine was talking to Misha as if everyday pleasantries were expected in a place like this with a man like Misha. Rimas watched and listened, curious.

Misha sat in a dining chair across from him at the low table with a hot mug of coffee and a cleaning kit before him. He released the magazine of his SIG Sauer pistol, pulled back the slide, and emptied the chambered round into his hand before answering her question in his usual still manner, blue eyes locking on without a blink. He spoke English.

"My rest was sufficient, thank you. No."

She interrupted, "I know how to clean a pistol."

"I am aware you do, but you may not touch one of ours. I hope that is clear. You may bring a chair and join us if it will help relieve your boredom, though my storytelling will likely make the condition worse."

Was the older man becoming—what was the English expression—mellow? Rimas watched him remove the slide and lay out the barrel and recoil spring.

What story?

"Welche Geschichte?" he asked out loud.

"Use English," said Misha. "Christine does not speak German. I was telling you about the girl Vasily met here in Montreal." He soaked a patch in solvent and pushed it through the barrel.

Christine dragged over a chair and sat. Rimas wished Jade would do the same and wondered why she did not. He watched her face as she cleared notebooks, coffee cans, and mugs from the island counter that separated the living room from the kitchen. She was paying too much attention to Skosh as she worked. Rimas scowled. What were they talking about?

"Who is Vasily?" Christine asked as if she had a right to a reply. To Rimas's surprise, after taking his time to consider his words, Misha answered.

"He was an original member of the team and also my friend since childhood."

"Team?"

Rimas was sure she knew about the team. She had called him an assassin in the park. He still found the word uncomfortable, or rather, the knowledge that it was accurate did not sit well with his ego. He liked to think he was a good man. How can a good man bring death to anyone, even an evil man, without sharing the evil?

Misha sent a bore brush down the SIG's barrel as he told her about Vasily, his Polish roots, his mathematical prowess, and his skill as a killer. Misha used the word fighter instead, but Rimas remembered talk of Vasily during his earliest training as a boy in Lithuania. Vasily Sobieski's name was whispered with awe in anti-Soviet circles. He was to be revered—and feared.

Rimas pulled a cloth out of the footlocker at his feet and polished the rifle he had just finished. Now, the name was becoming the basis of a lesson he did not yet understand. Why these stories from almost three decades back?

"I heard them call you Misha," said Christine. "Are you Russian?"

Misha's silent stare, just inside the safer edge of belligerence, meant he found her question impertinent. No, not impertinent.

She is interrogating him. She must be dirty.

Rimas became less bored.

"I am Austrian." Misha's tone was unfriendly.

"You were talking about Vasily's girlfriend." She prompted, pretending not to notice the chill, almost demanding an answer.

Definitely dirty. Also brave, or maybe just foolish.

Rimas raised an eyebrow as she tried to match the belligerence in Misha's stare. She failed and dropped her gaze first.

"Vasily had no skill in speaking to others, especially women," Misha continued. "He saw the world as a collection of numbers, geometrical figures, progressions made by factors and exponents in elegant sentences called formulae. A sentence of words held no depth in his mind, could never be a thing of beauty."

Rimas paused in his polishing. Was this why Misha kept telling him about Vasily—because he shared this trait? He rejected the idea. He would never be as good with numbers as he wanted to be, though he continued to try. He simply had no skill at stringing words, not in any of his four languages.

Misha continued. "Women sensed he was dangerous and often stayed away. If one came close, Vasily soon learned she wanted something from him. All he had for them was pain and death because it was all he knew, both giving and receiving. But he came to my house very young, and my family civilized him as well as they were able. He had his own moral code and adhered to the team's rules. Such rules can be important for those with the authority to use deadly force, wouldn't you agree, Lieutenant?"

"You have rules?"

The woman looked Misha in the eye.

Brave. Foolish. Dirty.

The two paused in mutual animosity.

"Don't you?"

Another pause. She looked down. "Of course."

Another victory for Misha, who ran a dry patch through the SIG's barrel. It looked clean to Rimas, but Misha pushed another before inspecting the frame.

Misha broke the silence. "Rules may protect an innocent against injury, but they do nothing to shield the guilty from damage."

Christine tilted her head and squinted. "I don't understand. Why would we want to protect the guilty?"

"Spoken like a policewoman who does not understand she is among the guilty. Every exercise of raw power, even without violence, changes you. You are not the same woman you were twenty-three years ago when you joined the police.

"Twenty-three years? How did you...?"

"We have a computer." Misha pointed to it with the slide in his hand.

Rimas watched Christine gain control of her surprise and force her face into the worldwide official expression of stern wariness adopted by all with the power to hurt you. He had been learning the same.

"I am allowed to use force in defense of myself and others," she said with a convinced tone. "I follow the rules. Are you saying I'm damaged anyway?"

"No. I say you are changed. Rules cannot stop change. Damage comes when you feel altered but do not like or understand it. Some become arrogant and cruel, others fearful and jumpy. Some shun all contact with people, others crave it. Vasily created a fantasy world where he had never been orphaned or tortured or taught to fight and, most of all, had never killed."

Rimas laid the rifle in its case and conducted an internal inventory. He was not jumpy or fearful and indeed not cruel. Arrogant? He had to admit that. Christine had noticed it. Fantasy? Surely not. What would he fantasize about?

The noise in the room increased. The babysitters brought in lunch from the caterers' truck. Jade, as usual, had large spoons ready to dish the food, paper plates and plastic utensils to receive it. She was perfect in every way, Rimas mused as he plotted to make sure she sat next to him as they ate.

"I have never killed and hope I never have to," said Christine.

Misha slipped the barrel and spring into the slide. "Not everyone who enters your job considers the possibility. They glory in power and noble purpose but never consider the smell of sweat or the desperate strain of failing muscles clinging to life without hope. Defeated foes bring no glory to their vanquishers, only the threat of vengeance. Look into the eyes of a soldier returning from combat, or better, a soldier dying on the battlefield."

Rimas pushed aside a memory of the mentor of his youth, Kestutis, dying in his arms.

The noise increased as Sergei turned from the computer and began joking with Steve. Christine looked down at her hands on her lap, then up at Misha. "You are quite the philosopher."

"No, just a killer." He said it quietly, throwing a glance in Rimas's direction. "My wife is the philosopher. Vasily was her first husband. He discovered that he wanted most to be with a woman who would support the fantasy of not being what he was. Shortly before he met her, he thought he had found his dream here in Montreal."

"What happened?"
He gave her a half smile. "He was wrong."

FOURTEEN

C hristine didn't buy it. Not any of it. They all had the look in their eyes, men with guns and extreme biceps who spoke too many languages. Even when they used English, it came out in indecipherable jargon. She should walk out. She should put them all under arrest and then walk out. *Where to?* She did not know where in Montreal Frank had brought her. A residential street of two-story rectangular brick boxes.

Skip the arrest; no jurisdiction. Where is my brain? Maybe walk out quietly when they aren't looking. At least, get to a phone.

She could find her way to the local Mountie station.

She surveyed the room. They made no sign of being impressed by her existence. Answers to her occasional questions came with minimal information, volunteering nothing. No facts advanced. Even Steve came downstairs and walked by her without his previous speculative *how-about-it?* glance. She felt more menace than flattery in his regard, but being a ghost was no fun at all, either. Even though no one looked at her, she knew they were all perfectly aware of her exact location. When she moved a hand to tighten her ponytail, Charlie and the Russian guy, Sergei, standing across the room at the coffee machine, paused their quiet conversation.

So Christine experimented. She moved cautiously toward the side door, concentrating on being as quiet as that guy, Charlie, though not expecting to reach his level of perfection. The so-called babysitters, the Feds as she called them, immediately looked her way. Frank's eyes bulged under raised brows. She calculated her chances in a sprint to the door—*nil*—and opted instead for more coffee. Charlie and Sergei moved away, still talking, not English.

I am a prisoner with coffee privileges.

Their discussion over, Charlie reappeared at her elbow like a specter, a malignant presence unseen but fully felt. She concentrated on pouring but contemplated throwing the pot at him.

"I wouldn't if I were you."

What the hell?

She hadn't even looked at him. She put the pot down and turned to face him. He spoke again.

"You don't know our capabilities, Christine. Best to go with the flow, as you Americans say."

The Russian guy, Sergei, approached again with a worried face.

"I need to call...."

He used English because, well, courtesy. These criminals had manners but no Algonquian languages. Not that Christine could boast about her fluency.

Charlie barked at him, "I asked you at lunch to look up the license number Skosh gave us. Have you?"

Sergei shuffled, needing movement to calm himself. "Please, Charlie. Very quick. She is having contractions. I worry."

"I do, too, about Mara, of course, but right now, about all of us. Go, do the search. First."

"She should not have kept this baby even though it is a son. It will kill her."

"I agree," Charlie said, visibly straining at tolerance. "My sister flirts with death at every opportunity. She has good doctors. Now, do as I say. No more discussion."

Christine cataloged the tension in their exchange, the family references, and the exchange of glances between Charlie and Mack. She knew she was again the topic of that silent communication. Mack holstered his re-assembled SIG, telegraphing with a glance in her direction an almost palpable distrust. Christine embraced invisibility again, reminding herself how good it was to be a ghost.

Steve walked up and handed her an empty mug. She looked down at the pot still in her hand, still tempting her to convert it into a weapon.

"I'd like a cup, too, if you don't mind," said Charlie. "While you're at it."

She put her mug on the counter. It would grow cold while she served them, but she took advantage of the chance to listen and learn.

"Sergei's losing it, Charlie. Is there any word from Theresa?"

Who the hell is Theresa?

Charlie closed his eyes momentarily. "Only with her usual, guarded medical-ese. Wait and see sort of thing. She won't say so, but it's not looking good." He took a deep sip of coffee.

Do these guys—should these guys—reproduce?

Charlie scowled at her as if he'd read her mind.

"He's a quivering bowl of pudding over this baby," said Steve. "He hasn't cleaned his Makarov since before we left. Rimas studies all that electronic shit. I'm glad you're letting me bring him with us tonight instead of Sergei. Don't give him any more pressure, Charlie. Not yet."

Charlie nodded. "We'll have a meeting as soon as he has a line on that neighbor. I will find a way to couch it without making it a slight to him."

Christine handed them their mugs robotically, wrapped in the cloak of invisibility afforded by simple service, barely breathing, and wondering when they would stop talking so freely in the presence of somebody they did not trust.

Steve's slow Texas drawl accompanied a half-smile. "I don't think he'll even notice, to tell you the truth. I don't get it. I've seen them in action together dozens of times. Never a glitch, even when she's beside him in a firefight. What is unhinging him?"

"A threat from an unknown direction?" Charlie looked up from a study of the liquid in his mug. "Casualties in action are one thing, but childbirth? I never considered it a factor until Theresa explained the danger back when Mara made the decision. I'm not used to the idea of losing her. She never lets me keep her out of the action on an op and made it clear this decision was only hers to make. She's right. The team can't share it any more than we can carry the baby. But I wish she didn't."

Steve drained his cup and glanced at the too-observant woman holding a coffee pot, a small dog at her feet. "Any sign of interest in the pooch?"

"Yes. We'll discuss it after you get back. That reminds me, we need you to bring back Jade's computer from the babysitters' house, too. We'll put it on the table next to Sergei's. Skosh will squawk. He won't be able to stop Sergei from watching her log in."

Charlie dropped a momentary delighted grin as he held out his cup for another refill, eyes suspicious and hooded.

As she drained the pot and made another, it occurred to Christine they spoke freely in front of her because the creature they wanted here was the dog, not her. They were making use of him. Fluffy couldn't repeat anything he heard, and they were confident in their ability to silence Christine—at will and for good.

FIFTEEN

"The dog was a pain in the ass. Just like she said he would be," Frank told Skosh as he handed him a damp cloth. "How did Christine do?"

Skosh could smell coconut oil and soap on the cloth as he buried his face in it, removing the camo paint after their nighttime excursion to retrieve the sensors. He shrugged. "She took the monitor from me and was gone before I jumped the fence. She's pretty fast." He turned the rag and gave his ears and neck the same treatment while watching the woman in question. Well, he had to admit he was watching Jade, who was helping Christine clean her face.

"How'd you do?" murmured Frank.

Skosh answered the same way. "I didn't kill anybody if that's what you're asking. Nobody did. For a change. I think the guy was out or asleep; the place was dark. Car was there, though. I don't know why I had to go. Too many cooks, in my mind. Could have been a disaster trying to get that many people to be-have like they're not there."

"I think that's why Charlie sent you. To find out if you can handle it. Did you pass?"

"God, I hope not. This job is shitty—thanks a lot for promoting me to it—but theirs is worse, and the last thing I want is a job offer from Charlie. Where do we sleep, by the way? Not on rotation with the team, I hope."

Frank ran fat fingers through the thin hair fringing his head. He gave a half-shrug, one shoulder only, be-fore answering. "The good news is there's an attic, and Jade was able to move a couple of old dressers and rig a sheet across the middle, so we can split evenly, men on one end, women on the other, team on the floor be-low. Bad news is spiders. Even worse, Jade says she's allergic, as in screaming bloody terror allergic. So far, she's kept it together. Accommodation-wise, it could be worse."

Another thing we have in common. Skosh sighed as he watched Jade set up her keyboard and screen in the space Sergei had cleared for her on the table. She plugged them into the CPU tower on the floor. The machines stood back to back to shield their hands from each other's sight as they typed. Skosh approved. He had gone to a lot of trouble to scrub the team's fingers out of The Section's file system.

"What about Christine? How is she with spiders?"

"I guess they call state cops troopers for a reason. She's made of granite."

Skosh nodded. "That's why Charlie doesn't trust her."

"Which is why he sent Sergei with her. I'm sure there was a clear order in the event of a misstep."

"Yeah. No doubt."

She was sitting in a chair near the front door, face free of camo paint, hugging Fluffy. Skosh heard her tell Jade the dog had to go outside soon.

A dog needs to lift his leg and it takes a fucking strategic campaign to get him to a tree, in this case, a bush by the garage's back door, led by a none-too-happy Rimas. Skosh always smiled when Rimas scowled like that. He walked over to Charlie, who stood looking over Sergei's shoulder at the computer screen.

"Charlie, how about we make it clear to everybody that the attic is babysitter territory? Team members should steer clear. It'll make up for the loss of our safehouse."

He had tried to make his tone friendly, casual, without agenda. The ice-blue stare from Charlie told him he failed, and the answer confirmed it.

"The comfort and security of you babysitters have never been high on my list of concerns, Skosh. But if it makes you feel any better, Rimas will be too busy this trip."

He dragged out the word busy, squinting one eye as he tilted his chin into his trademark arrogant challenge, then instantly softened it. "Why don't you fix the situation with Jade?" he demanded.

Skosh couldn't hide his surprise. He sputtered, "I can't..."

"Yeah, yeah, I know all those English words like taking advantage and fraternization that you people complain about, but couldn't you just marry her? I know it's old-fashioned, but she's probably worth the risk."

Of course, she's worth the risk.

He glanced inadvertently at Rimas coming through the door with a relieved-looking rat terrier. And, of course, Charlie caught it.

"Don't worry about the Rimas equation, either, Skosh. My father will take care of that side of it. You just ask her. Soon. Then, concentrate on getting us all out of this op alive."

SIXTEEN

Christine rubbed at the residual night paint near her ear while she processed the situation as Frank explained it. The paint would never come off. She had been glad to help cart things from the other house. It relieved the boredom. But she didn't trust the jumpy Russian who took the CPU from her only to leave her hoisting the heavier monitor with a keyboard and mouse balancing on top of it. He'd kept one hand free, she noticed. The one closest to her. And not so as to be helpful.

Steve of the melting brown eyes droned on about names she never wanted to know. She sat on another uncomfortable chair in a roomful of criminals, wanting to casually walk over to that phone on the wall, wondering how she was going to share a room with three people, two of them men. Not a room, a sleeping space, they said. Four-hour shifts. Sleeping only. That had been emphasized, with glances to both her and Jade, like all hanky-panky is ultimately the responsibility of the female. A snort of disgust escaped her, but her continued invisibility covered it.

There had been a time when all these fit younger men would be tempting, especially Steve, closest to her age, with his invitational glances, but the need to survive without the benefit of information occupied her now. She was too busy trying to figure out what the hell was going on.

She heard the words 'white supremacy'. *Shit. They are Nazis.* Then, she heard 'target' and then 'civil rights activist' in close succession and let out another disgusted snort. None of this made sense.

Mack interrupted Steve's narrative. "I believe the police lieutenant has a comment."

All attention swiveled to her. "What? No, please go on."

"A question then?" His blue eyes fixed on her, compelling an answer.

"I just don't understand any of it, that's all." She held Fluffy a little more tightly in her lap, gathering from him the courage to go out telling the truth.

Frank didn't rescue me; he captured me.

"I'm not armed and I'm outnumbered," she said, "but if you think I will stand by while you murder a civil rights leader... I'm a cop and I'll find a way to take you down."

From the grave if I have to.

Fluffy whined. She loosened her grip. The room became silent. Even the computer's fan seemed muted. Steve rolled his eyes and tilted his head in the traditional gesture of male arrogance. She tried to think of a witty way to spit defiance.

"Don't think your Texas accent will make an ally out of me, cowboy," she said.

"I don't have an accent."

"You do, too."

He put on a patient look and narrowed his eyes. "I don't have an accent that would confuse anybody speaking English, even somebody from Vermont. I don't know what unknown region you're inhabiting right now, Loootenant, but here on earth, in this here room, we're talking about our target, not our target's target."

It took less than half a breath to process his words before the blood rushed into her face.

Charlie entered the exchange with a note of venom. "Now that we have established you were not listening, Christine, I will briefly repeat Steve's more important points. I trust you can understand *my* accent."

His accent was all American, even if he wasn't, and he waited for an answer. She nodded ever so slightly to keep the tears of embarrassment from spilling down her cheeks, feeling everybody watching, willing them to look elsewhere, away from her false accusation—in her family, it was the worst of all sins—wishing for a wormhole to crawl into.

"Shane Chatham is our target," Charlie said smoothly. "He is the American you saw shoot a Canadian black man this morning. Our information is that he is using the name Smitty and is here to take out Sidney Alcoa, an American indigenous rights activist. Alcoa will arrive in Montreal tomorrow to give a speech the next day and receive an award honoring him for his work with local tribes. We hope to stop Chatham. We also hope to learn a few things. The incident you witnessed in the park has complicated both goals." He paused and raised one eyebrow. "Questions?"

She risked more embarrassment, thinking it couldn't be worse, but held her breath, expecting it to be.

"Why can't I stay in the other house?"

Away from you.

"We are getting to that."

When his gaze shifted to Sergei, Christine felt unnoticed again. She breathed.

"Tell us about the license plate, Sergei."

Christine considered the man as he turned from his computer keyboard. She would not want to meet any of these guys in a dark alley, but this one especially. The compact, muscular build suggested speed, and his almost transparent eyes looked right through you.

He had stood very still next to her at the fence where Skosh handed them the computer parts. Even in the dark, she felt the attention he paid to her movements, watching her hands with an assessing eye. The memory made her shiver as he answered with a thick Russian accent. She looked away and noticed Rimas watching her. He had seen the shiver.

"The plate is from New York," said Sergei. "The car belongs to a man who calls himself Paul Smith. Officially, he has an import business. He is not related to anyone with the name registered to the house where he is staying. He lives in Plattsburgh, New York, and frequently comes to Montreal for business. The house is listed as his destination every time he enters the country."

"Fake name on the lease," drawled Steve. "Any other signs?"

"Yes. There are two million Americans of that name."

"So it's common. What else?"

"I have a small indication that it may be an alias. There are several Smiths in Interpol database, but one is suspected to operate out of New York."

"Operate what?" asked Charlie.

"I do not know. I could not access the individual file. I also do not know why Interpol lists him. We need better access."

All heads turned to Skosh standing by the coffee machine.

"Jade is still setting up her system," he said, pointing to her as she knelt under the table, running a cable.

"Have you heard from the Canadians?" Charlie asked him.

"I have. They have light surveillance on what looks like a safehouse near the park. That's where the two watchers Rimas noticed entered. They were careful to dry clean their route."

"But unsuccessful." Charlie smiled. "If they turn up at Smith's safehouse, we will have stumbled into the network we're looking for. A useful coincidence. There is no sign we're blown."

"There is yet another coincidence," said Mack. "Smith is an old name."

"I am sure it has a noble history," said Charlie, "but I agree with Sergei it is probably an alias in this case."

"That is what I am referring to—an alias that has been used in this area for a long time."

"But he is American," said Sergei, "not from Montreal."

"It's a very common name, Papa, easy to use as an alias."

The muscles of Misha's jaw tightened under forced patience. "If you will listen…" He glared them into respectful silence before continuing.

"When we were here soon after the October Crisis almost three decades ago, we encountered a babysitter from Colorado calling himself Gary Smith. We watched him meet a specialist from New Hampshire, also named Smith, who had already taken out a Canadian press agent instrumental in changing public sentiment against the FLQ.

"Darren Smith was after an FLQ informant who was due to receive a light sentence for his role in the incident. He had taken no part in the killing and was now trading information for a few years of freedom. We were too late to stop the revenge assassination of the press agent, but the informant had more information to give, so we were asked to stay."

"Who were you working for?" asked Skosh.

"Us," answered Frank. "They worked for us. We wanted to know who deployed Gary Smith's specialists. Charlemagne was the perfect choice to find out. The Canadians blessed our proposal, just like they have this time. They—and we—were more than curious to know who wanted these two dead, I mean, aside from friends of the other government official who died in the crisis two months before."

"I'm seeing a parallel," said Skosh as he took the chair under the cat poster near Jade. "We need to know who Chatham is reporting to. We know he's not solo. The common names suggest a pattern."

Misha nodded. "In the earlier op during the '70s, we began surveillance of Darren. Frank worried because, on paper, the two Smiths had come from different American states."

Frank dabbed ineffectually with a paper napkin at coffee that stained his white shirt."It suggested a nationwide link," he said. "Then, the watchers I hired found a woman also called Smith. It looked like Darren and Gloria were an item."

Rimas wrinkled his brow and tilted his head back at the mention of the name.

Skosh shrugged, walked to the sink, and brought Frank a damp rag for the coffee stain. "So maybe they were married?"

"No," said Mack. "Her passport gave her an address in Wisconsin."

Frank nodded. "Now we had three people named Smith from three states. Using the same name must be a conceit of the organization, a mark of membership. It concerned us, and rightly so, as it turned out."

"Today, we have two Smiths," said Mack, "our target and this unexpected neighbor in the duplex."

Christine leaned forward in her chair. "Wait, earlier, you said your target's name is Chatham."

. . .

Misha studied her face, surprised at her determined grasp of information amid the chaos that threatened her. Her expression was serious, slightly puzzled, and fully engaged in the conversation, unlike Gloria Smith, who had feigned ignorance. And Vasily had fallen for it. This one was taking an alternate tack—if she was dirty. She might not be. It was theoretically possible for a woman to be intelligent and free of guile. He had

73

learned to appreciate these traits in the women at home, though at the same time, they could be irritating as hell.

"We intercepted a message from him to a superior. He signed it Smitty," said Michael.

"A message?" She tilted her head sideways.

It described the murder you witnessed." He paused, also studying her. "And included a description of you. And of the dog."

"Oh." She parted her lips slightly, dropped her gaze to stare inward, and said slowly, "But you intercepted it. So there's still only one guy—this Chatham character—that I need to worry about."

When nobody answered after a few beats, she added, "Right?"

"We put the message back, and this evening, two men near the park noticed you. They show signs they are in the game."

Misha watched her critically and was gratified to see her eyes open wide. It appeared sudden, automatic, a genuine reaction to bad news.

"Why?" she croaked, her face now pale.

Michael sat back in his easy chair and held his empty mug in Skosh's direction. Skosh got up to fill it. "Because, Lieutenant, we don't want just Chatham. We are after the entire organization."

"But if he sent a message about me, then the whole organization is after me." She emphasized the last word and pointed to herself. "You're using me to ferret out an entire gang?"

Steve answered her. "Pretty much. Yeah."

Color came back to her cheeks; her eyes narrowed with anger. "Can I at least be armed? I saw that footlocker over there. You guys have plenty of firepower to share."

Amazing. A dangle who knew her danger, consented to it, though grudgingly, and refused to be passive about it. The team and babysitters all turned to his son for his answer.

"No." Cold and still as ever.

The woman's face blanched again, and Michael broke precedent by giving her the unusual benefit of a more complete explanation.

"They would notice you're armed and be suspicious of a trick. As are we."

"Me? I'm the cop here. You guys are... I don't know what you are, but I don't kill people willy-nilly like...."

"But you make assumptions willy-nilly, don't you?"

"What? Oh." She took a deep breath and blushed red again. Misha approved. She had the decency to be embarrassed. It seemed another genuine trait. If she was dirty, then she was, at least, a better actress than Gloria.

...

They were still talking when Jade told Christine it was her turn in the sack. She and Fluffy made their way up the attic stairs and onto a narrow cot surrounded by broken furniture and hanging blankets. A single bulb hanging from a hook in the rafters lit the space but did not interfere with Christine's ability to sleep within seconds.

Two minutes later, it seemed, Jade poked her shoulder with a finger, and Fluffy growled from under the blanket.

"My turn, Christine. Go downstairs."

"Already? How long…"

"You had four hours. Now let me have mine. You get to hear what the targets are up to. The Smith guy is awake, and Sergei is putting him on speaker. Lucky you. Fill me in on it in four hours, no sooner."

SEVENTEEN

It began with a radio squawk, shrill, full of static. The receiver squelched. The audience, Charlemagne, with their babysitters and prisoner, as she insisted on calling herself, had arranged itself in uncomfortable chairs, forming a lopsided arc around the computers.

Sergei switched the audio to the main speakers and played the recorded file. The caller's initial cough may or may not have carried over the air. It depended on whether he had pressed talk. Their touch was in the inside wall of the duplex, giving them more information about his state than he gave over the radio.

```
Listen, Ga⁀y, I gotta talk to
him. Can you give him your
brick? And leave the room. It's
confidential.
```

He slurped a drink. Probably coffee.

```
Smith here.
```

A squawk cut short, almost as short as the clipped words.

The man in the house cleared his throat.

```
Boss, this is Paul.
Authenticate.
Liberty.
```

Not very original.

```
Go ahead.
```
The correct answer, though. The man cleared his throat again. And coughed.
```
Um... I'm not questioning the or-
der, you understand. He's been
out of control for some time. I
just don't know how to find him.
Also, there is another develop-
ment.
```
Another slurp and seven steps on a wood floor. Pause. Seven more. Pacing?
```
His tradecraft has always been
good. You'll have to lure him.
What development?
```
The static on Smith's radio was heavy, but the team's signal from the house was clear. Paul took a deep, audible breath, hissing air into his lungs, no doubt keeping his finger off the talk button to hide the hesitation. When it came at last, his voice sounded careful, reluctant.
```
I think the landlord rented out
the other side of the safehouse.
It's a duplex, so a security
risk. Maybe I should move. About
Chatham. Last I heard [static]
Last I heard, he was looking for
a fucking dog. I heard we're
looking, too. I've been told
it's your order. You took four
of my watchers who should be
checking out these new tenants
next door. I don't know if I'll
have enough watchers to catch
Alcoa's arrival. We should have
rented both houses.
```

The boss spoke in extra decibels.

> The house has always been se-
> cure, and it was expensive
> enough on its own. Perfect loca-
> tion. Any tenants next door will
> be short-term. We made sure. And
> say target, not the name. Get
> some fucking discipline, Paul.
> You're as bad as Shane. We've
> seen the dog. We'll deliver his
> quarry to you as soon as it can
> be arranged. You take it from
> there. He thinks he has to elim-
> inate her before he can work.

The pacing stopped momentarily.

> The dog's a female?

The radio exploded again.

> No, you fucking moron. Its owner
> is. Once you have her, we'll
> make sure he hears of it. He'll
> come to you. Then you do what's
> necessary. I'm done with him.

> What about her?

> She's a brown nobody. Do what
> you want after I come and see if
> she's worth my time. Control the
> goons. I'll want her fresh, if
> at all.

> And the target? If Shane's too
> dead, who…?"

```
To  be  determined.  Get  some
sleep.  And  don't  let  me  hear
your  voice  again  until  you've
done your fucking job. Over.
```

Charlie put down the headphones while Sergei turned off the tape, both eyebrows raised expectantly.

"Go, wake up Rimas. Have him meet me in the car. No listeners."

EIGHTEEN

M aybe he was too fond of kissing her. Perhaps that was why Michael's order made Rimas uncomfortable. It seemed a sneaky thing to do, but then, being a sneak was his job. To her, it would seem like a betrayal, he knew, and he hoped rescuing Fluffy at the last minute would help her forgive it. If the plan worked, he wanted another kiss, a real one this time, not part of a legend. If she lived. Insufficient as a substitute for Jade, but the woman could kiss, and he craved the touch of her softness.

The plan was simple, his part in it, flawless. Rimas took the leash from her, letting Fluffy pull him, straining towards intriguing smells at the gutter, creating a gap of only a few inches between them. He pretended not to notice the two unknowns who stepped up behind her, then moved to either side. She yelled his name only briefly, no doubt silenced by whatever weapon they showed her quietly in the crowd.

Rimas stopped in the gutter and watched her dark ponytail disappear in the crowds moving away down the sidewalk. Fluffy lifted his leg at the curb.

"I've got them," said Steve's voice in his ear.

Rimas jumped onto the curb in time to avoid being hit as Skosh slowed a muddy dark green Peugeot beside him. He picked up Fluffy and folded his six-foot frame into the passenger seat.

"Turning right," Michael murmured through their earbuds minutes later. Skosh pulled into position, allowing the silver Ford that carried Christine to pass him in heavy traffic on René Levesque Boulevard. Misha turned the Mercedes sedan behind them from a side street. They followed two cars back, took a right turn after the Ford, but continued straight when it turned again. Misha turned after them and followed until they hit Rene Levesque again and turned right a third time to continue in the original direction. He turned left as Jade took up the slow chase in an old, red Mitsubishi Steve had stolen in Laval. Steve was her passenger, probably making her uncomfortable. Rimas grimaced at the thought.

"They're still dry cleaning," Steve announced to everybody's ear. "These guys are good. Looks like they're headed for the Victoria Bridge. Need somebody on the other side of it."

Misha used the Champlain bridge to meet them as they turned left off the Victoria on route 132, heading north along the river only long enough to turn back across again, this time using the Jacques Cartier bridge, where Michael picked up the Smith car on the other side. Satisfied they had shaken any surveillance, Christine's abductors took their time crossing the island and heading into the residential neighborhoods of Laval. Michael and his team took turns keeping a light surveillance behind.

Skosh and Rimas were turning toward the safehouse when Steve's voice came over the network.

"You were right, Charlie. They're pulling into the house next door to the babysitters' and there's no sign of another visitor."

"Not yet, but give them time," said Michael, his voice as cool as ever, as if Christine had endless time. Like success or failure, life or death were all equally unremarkable.

"I will hear when they come in," said Sergei, back in the safehouse manning the computer and listening equipment.

Computers, plural, Rimas corrected to himself. Nothing Jade could have done to protect her system would keep Sergei out now. He glanced at Skosh, saw the seething scowl, and looked away to hide his smile.

Sergei held his mic to the speaker coming from the taps he had on Paul Smith. They listened in on the initial beating Christine was getting, then the first shouted questions, some slaps, grunts, one or two screams—from her interrogator, not from her. But the worst part, for Rimas anyway, was the laughter as they called her names he did not understand. In between the blows.

"It seems another coincidence that they are using that safehouse," said Misha, "but at least she has not blown us."

NINETEEN

It wasn't the first blow that made her decide. It was the first words from the older specimen with a crew cut wearing a football jersey.

"You're not white, but you're not black, either. What are you?"

"Human."

The answering blow was substantial. It cut her lip on a tooth.

"Don't smart mouth me again, squaw, or I'll split the other lip."

She believed him. And now she credited Charlie, too. These were the Nazis, not Charlie and his team. They were just the bastards who had let this happen to her. There was no way Rimas didn't know they were taking her. He had to be obeying an order from Charlie.

"My boyfriend will be looking for me."

She hoped it was true, that it was part of the plan.

"Boyfriend! Who'd fuck a mutt like you?"

Loud laughter from the two goons who had brought her there, then racial epithets and comments about her skin, her face, and private body parts.

"I know, right Paul?" said the greasy-haired one. "He's kissed her a bunch of times. And he's a white guy. Go figure." He handed crew-cut Paul a picture."

We kinda got into the role…

He looked from the photo to her face, studying it. He glanced away quickly to break their brief eye contact like it burned his retina. "Isn't he a little young for you?"

If our ages were reversed, you wouldn't even think it, let alone say it, you son of a bitch.

But this was not the time, and these were not the guys to discuss gender inequalities. She sucked on her bloody lip.

"Somebody's looking for you, bitch," said Paul, "but it ain't your boyfriend."

"Who?" The question escaped her because of genuine curiosity. She did not expect a reply.

"Let's just say it's somebody you met in the park yesterday. He thinks he's gotta do damage control to stop you telling lies about what you think you saw."

"So you're a friend of his?" So much for Frank's concern for her safety. She should have said no.

"You might say that." The man kept engaging and avoiding her stare as if both fascinated and repelled by her eyes.

"I've already given his description to the cops," she said. "He should get as far away as possible, as soon as possible."

"That's not our plan."

"I thought you said you were his friends."

The man nodded, still avoiding eye contact. "As long as he does as he's told. He thinks solving the problem of you will fix the problem he's caused with us. He's wrong."

"Then you're not going to let him kill me?"

"I didn't say that."

How did that early morning walk in a park to let her dog take a piss turn her into a worm on so many different hooks, all of them criminal? She found herself choosing sides in this deadly game and wondered when Charlemagne would rescue her. How they would rescue her.

If they would rescue her.

TWENTY

"Do you plan to retrieve the policewoman?" Misha asked his son.

The two sat in the sedan inside the closed garage of their safehouse. Summer heat, magnified by closed windows, brought out a healthy sweat. Both men were unaffected by minor discomforts. Michael used the car as a private place for the team to meet, guaranteed out of earshot of the babysitters. He paused to consider an answer to Misha's question.

"Papa, you've anticipated the reason I asked you here. I could use your perspective. Rimas is struggling. Sergei is a mess. I can't have two of them unreliable. Ever since that op in the Congo last year, the servants at home tell me Rimas's nightmares are more frequent. To disappoint him about Jade now..."

"You agreed, Michael, before we left for this op. Better a disappointment on this trip than disaster within months. You know your stepmother is right. Jade cannot live with us. Rimas will adjust."

Michael sucked in air through clenched teeth. "I did not let Rimas listen to all of the woman's interrogation. It should not mean anything to him, but he took extra time on that last kiss before letting them take her. He keeps looking at me with moonstruck concern. How does he get attached so easily?"

Misha turned his head away to hide a smile, but Michael saw it in the wing mirror.

"I got over it, Papa."

"Which one? The one you married after nine years or the other?"

Michael ignored the uncomfortable reminder about the crush who had tried to kill him and kept the conversation on his excellent wife. "You often say Theresa is perfect. She has always been...."

"Theresa is Frank's daughter. She is accustomed to men with nightmares, who explode without warning. And you both had time to mature in those years. Rimas is a puppy, like Vasily was in 1971, happy to be petted by any woman—until he learned to fear treachery from the softest quarter. Jade will never understand the likes of us."

"She will have to if Skosh makes his move."

"Skosh has killed, but he is not committed to a specialist life."

"I admit I could use him. He and Steve would be highly effective together on the team."

Misha chuckled. "They speak the same language. Liberal use of the f-word with an occasional noun."

Michael returned the chuckle with a guffaw. "Imagine the two of them at the dinner table with Great Aunt Battle Axe."

They indulged in a laugh until Misha sobered long enough to say, "I have told you repeatedly, do not call her that out loud. You will let it slip at the worst moment."

But the image was too much for both of them, and they gave themselves up to a few seconds of full belly laughs until Michael sighed.

"I have to retrieve the woman, don't I, Papa?"

"You do." Misha laid his head back against the headrest and shifted in his seat to ease the injured hip.

K.A. Bachus

"I'm not concerned about Chatham," said Michael. "He's a dead man the minute they lay eyes on him. They'll do that part of our job for us. But this guy Paul Smith is calling somebody 'boss.' I need that one. He's also using the name Smith. I can't ask Jade and Sergei for a simple computer search; there are too many with that name. Skosh says his government wants the whole network, or at least as much of it as we can find, and especially the money source."

Misha took a deep breath, eyes closed, chin up. Michael took advantage of the silence to solidify the decision that had formed in his mind. It was always easier to decide after speaking the problem aloud, even if no one was listening, and in this case, he had the best listener possible.

"The timing must be perfect. Who should I send, Papa?" He struggled to strip the whine out of his voice. This part of the decision always made him uncomfortable. To play with his own chance of survival was one thing. To weight the odds against others...

Misha's chin came down, and he turned his head to look at his son. "Rimas, of course."

Michael nodded. "But the Smiths must not die. I need them to lead us into the network. Rimas cannot manage it alone, and Steve is coordinating the search for the man they call boss."

"Smith's watchers need not live."

"True. But I cannot leave the management of Sergei to Steve. The word 'fuck' does not soothe him, though he uses plenty of it himself in Russian."

"Then send Rimas. I will run point for him."

Michael dropped his chin, surprised. "But your retirement...."

86

"Do not tell your stepmother. She gave me a task to do. It is no business of hers how I fulfill it. Rimas will retrieve the dangle. I will run point, and that is the end of it."

TWENTY-ONE

They drove past the Paul Smith safehouse in the babysitters' old beater of a Peugeot, parked it three houses down, and walked back casually. Misha deliberately emphasized his limp. An injured man does not look dangerous.

"You did not bring your cane," said Rimas. He remembered his transmitter was on, grimaced in shame at the mistake, and became silent as they approached the short walkway to the door.

...

Skosh felt used again. Okay, he'd been promised there wouldn't be any action. He appreciated that. What bothered him was the way they treated him. He preferred insults. Not only had the team become comfortable with him, but he also was getting used to it. His relationship with Steve was now a way too cozy camaraderie like it had been when they were both babysitters working for Frank. Back in the day.

Charlie's voice came through his earbud. "Move the signs."

Skosh stepped out with two orange plastic barrels. Moving slowly, he placed them evenly across the beginning of the street. He took his time attaching a cable to each barrel and unfurling a sign reading 'road closed.'

Sergei's voice: "I estimate one minute."

Skosh tried to look busy for that minute, making a meal of unfolding a sandwich board, placing it facing the wrong direction, correcting himself, letting it fall, picking it up, and holding up the detour arrow just as the car approached.

It wasn't the car they were looking for. It was full of young women talking and laughing.

Radio silence reigned. Another car approached. Skosh found something else wrong with the sandwich sign, picked it up, and put it down again. Memorized the license plate before the car turned on the detour. Spoke it quietly into the live mic at his throat. Sergei copied.

...

Paul Smith grimaced at the cold coffee in his cup. Bad enough to play hurry up and wait with the twits the boss had hired for this gig. He had worked with Canadians before and expected better. It didn't surprise him then when they admitted they were from Iowa. Damn. If you want us to act for you, the least you can do is supply the manpower, don't you think? Not a couple of hicks who lust after raping a half-breed and can't stop talking about it. Disgusting.

The boss was on his way and would, no doubt, take matters, and the woman, of course, into his own hands, then let Chatham come get her. Paul would complete the picture with a neat nine-millimeter hole in his head. The boss would be happy. The allies would worry about the objective, and he would wind up having to complete the mission. And not get paid for it.

Effective management was not a Smith strong-point. Chatham had been a wrong choice from the get-go. Too damaged by action in Bosnia.

Paul sat on the sofa, musing into his cold mug.

These two trolls were Americans, but not Smiths. One watcher—was his name Talon?—sat in a corner on the floor. The other, the one who went by the name White came out of the kitchen where he had ostensibly checked the prisoner, and by God, that better be all he did. There was a sound at the front door, and White walked toward it to open it. Must be the boss. He was running late.

Blood went everywhere. It sprayed. The guy with the knife stepped aside like he knew how to avoid it. Of course he did. Paul had begun to connect dots in the silent chaos in front of him and recognized a pro. He heard the pop-zip and felt, rather than saw, the man in the corner slump over. He looked into the barrel of a suppressed pistol, no bigger than a competition .22. He raised his eyes to meet a pair of dark blues in a young face, implacably set, raising one brow in question.

Involuntarily, Paul glanced at the kitchen door. Knife-man moved toward it, limping.

Dark Blue motioned for him to lie face down on the floor, and he complied with alacrity. He heard movements around him, saw the nicely creased summer wool pant leg of knife guy, and enjoyed relief at having his wrists tied painfully behind his back. It beat a fast bullet to the head—hands down. Then he remembered the boss should be on his way.

Relief vanished.

TWENTY-TWO

C hristine bent over the toilet as Jade kindly held her hair back. Only a few ounces of bile hit the water despite the mighty heaving that wracked her. She felt finished, empty, no longer sick, only tired. When she stood and turned to the door, she noticed the bloody footprints she had made, looked down to see blood on her bare feet in ruined sandals, and barfed again. Nothing came though, just a thin dribble down her chin. Jade handed her a towel.

"I'm a cop. I have seen worse," she told Jade. "I've seen car accidents you wouldn't believe. I've seen fights. I don't know why...."

"Because they accumulate," Jade said, filling a glass at the sink and handing it to her. "Just sip it. You need to watch for dehydration but don't push it. These things add up. The first time I saw it, I was so numb; I watched Mack use his knife and really didn't know what was happening, so I could shove it to one side of my brain and not look at it. But every time we're on an op and something happens that I can't avoid, it gives me more understanding and makes me sicker, even when it's not as bad as that first time. Hard to explain."

Christine took a sip and nodded as she swallowed. "When Mack cut the ropes on my wrists, I saw the knife in his hand as he helped me up. There was blood. Only a little, and some on his cuff. Then he took me out the front door, and there was this thing, this pale lump wearing blue jeans and this large pool of it, and I'm not even wearing socks. He made me keep walking. I'm so empty now. I wasn't then."

Jade took a clean washcloth from a stack on the vanity, wet it, and handed it to her. Christine wiped her face and sat down on the toilet seat to clean her feet while Jade washed her sandals in the sink. She told herself over and over again that now the squelching with each step was just water. It helped tame the threat of more dry heaves. When Rimas paused beside Frank at the coffee machine and looked at her, she felt an ounce of relief that this beautiful young man had not been the one with the knife, but it came with a pound of anger, and she headed toward him to share it.

"What the hell did you think you were doing? Why did you let them take me?"

He simply looked straight at her, no expression, a studied, practiced non-expression. It chilled her anger enough to make her find her answer.

"You were ordered," Christine said softly, with a defeated voice. She glanced over at Charlie. He stood next to Sergei, holding one of a set of headphones up against his right ear. Tape reels turned on a machine next to Sergei's computer. He met her glare and returned it with indifference. She shuddered and turned to Frank.

"What ...?" She could hardly get it out; the thought was too painful. "What happened to Fluffy?"

Frank grimaced at the clear, sinking tone in her question despite the noise in the room. She wondered if he had been waiting for it and expected terrible news. Probably, they used this guy for things like that. He was too old and fat to be one of them. He'd be an arranger instead of an enforcer, all smooth talking at high speed, with adrenaline. She braced herself for devastation.

"He's in the attic," he said, bulging eyes bloodshot from lack of sleep like all the rest. "He didn't want anything to do with me or Sergei and acted pretty unmanageable about it." There was resentment in his voice.

"I don't hear him." She whispered it as if that would quiet the room enough to amplify any remaining whimpers.

Frank shook his head. "He's been quiet for a couple of hours now."

"What did... did you...?

He shook his head again. "He bit Sergei, but not me."

Fluffy was never silent.

Paralyzed by the realization that her sanity depended on a ten-pound rat terrier, Christine took in her surroundings in three-dimensional high-contrast reality mode. She heard the noise of voices, heavy footsteps on an old wooden subfloor, the computers, a printer, and a radio squawking random static. The squalor of spilled food and oil-soaked gun patches next to every chair, wet coffee filters filling the sink, and the smell. Everybody stank now. She knew she did. Only Jade didn't. Though she was just as marooned without luggage as Christine, she had a perfume sample in her pocket.

Fluffy could blur a reality illuminated by the blood she had stepped in. He kept her whole every time she remembered her son. Fluffy was there when she opened a letter from the man who had promised before God to love and cherish her for all eternity, a letter full of threats, full of ways he would kill her. It was the need to protect that small furry body looking up at her with a face full of concern that gave her the courage to fight, to file the complaint and follow up, and show up in court to obtain a restraining order. Her ex quickly disobeyed it, of course, and now would never be eligible for parole. In the meantime, ordinary peace, quiet, and Fluffy had saved her life.

Fluffy and her in a one-bedroom, third-floor walk-up at the top of a Victorian farmhouse badly in need of paint. That was home. How could she go back there without him? How could she spend even five more minutes in this place without him?

"I will take you up there."

She heard the voice, its accented low pitch; what was his language again? Did he say Lithuanian? Where, exactly, was that? She looked up. He was so very tall. She had no power to move her feet. He put his hand on her shoulder.

"Come."

He stepped behind her and pushed gently. She turned to look up at him again. He tried again, and her feet began to obey her.

Two narrow flights of stairs ended at that rough plywood door; all around it a musty smell and still no sound, only the activity on the ground floor. Rimas reached the handle from behind her and opened it.

Fluffy launched himself into her arms, wiggled free, and fell to the floor, shrieking with joy, his entire back end wagging the skinny little half-tail at its end. She fell with him, not worried about the drops of happy pee he had sprinkled. He licked her face. She would have held him, but he could not be still or silent. He licked her face again, no doubt to taste the salt in her tears, then ran an obstacle course at top speed, leaping from cot to cot, jumping to catch the dividing curtain with his teeth and hang from it for an instant.

Rimas stood with his back to the door, watching. Christine stood up and faced him, cheeks wet, eyes still brimming. "I thought...."

His brow wrinkled into a vee at the bridge of his nose. "We are not monsters."

She kissed him. He kissed back. She accepted the depth of that kiss, sank into its intimacy, and returned it with every emotion inside her until he was inside her, where she needed him so badly to be. Hasty, maybe, a bit of a fumble here and there, always where the fumbling did the most good. Her nervous system kicked into overdrive. Every touch sent her to the mountain, and she stayed there a long, long time, savoring wave after wave at the pinnacle. A feast granted when she was starved for a simple touch.

...

At first, Fluffy wanted to protect her, but she wouldn't let him. He tried, but there was no room for him on the narrow cot. Then, he was jealous. She belonged to him, and this man was touching her, and she spoke sharply when he tried to make him stop. He found a shoe that smelled like another man, the one who had brought him up here to shut him away from her. It was brown and had laces.

He settled under the cot for a satisfying chew.

TWENTY-THREE

"Do you still think she may be dirty?" said Misha after a long sip of coffee.

Michael set down his headphones on the table next to Sergei and shook his head. "No, we heard all of it. She had opportunities to burn us and plenty of provocation. You saw the bruises. She held her own. For the most part, Lieutenant Barton is who she says she is. She may have a reason we don't yet know to do something stupid, but when Smith's boss rescues him, we can flip on the main speaker and let her hear it.

"I suspect she may be useful in more ways than as a dangle," said Misha. "She knows her way around a firearm, but I still would not give her a weapon. It is strange that Smith's boss has not returned after our detour."

Michael nodded. "But the flies are already in residence," he said, "and having a party."

Misha surveyed the room as it filled and became busier and louder. Frank put a large fan near the door to the garage, where a steep flight of steps descended into an unfinished basement. The door was open. If you stepped near it, you felt the cooler air from below that Frank was trying to circulate, but mostly, the fan just added a hot wind.

"When we were here in 1971, it was winter. We struggled to stay warm."

Michael smiled. "You're still not sure of her, are you?"

Misha answered slowly. "When you see too many coincidences among a great many unknowns, disaster is not far behind."

"You said you thought Gloria was dirty. Was she?"

Misha nodded.

"Then you took her out?"

"No." Misha gazed at his son, his firstborn, the hope of his youth who had turned out better than his father but at the wrong thing. "You know our psychology, how close we are to madness, especially in the moment of peril. Vasily was closer to it than most. He could easily have become like Chatham. He could blow the op. He nearly did. Chatham's team will delete him, but Vasily was my friend from the time I was five years old. I could not."

Michael's jaw gaped, surprised at his father's memory of the man he had loved as a child.

"What did you do, Papa?"

"I did not know what to do at first. It took me time to devise a plan. I needed Vasily to become rational again. I waited for his madness to move him to a place of reality. It was more difficult to control myself, to not interfere. It worked, but only barely."

Michael watched the staircase. Rimas had not yet come down.

Misha calculated the time it should take to retrieve a dog from the third floor and smiled. "I hope when we are home— if we come home," he said, "no one will let slip my role in Christine's rescue. I can explain my reasons to Alex, but would rather not. There was justification. She will say nothing, but her strange notions of fate and responsibility will make her regret she talked me into joining this trip. I do not want her to regret anything."

Especially not me.

"It is a perilous time to fix this problem, Papa, but I agree there seems no other way. And it must be done. At home, Rimas is too comfortable to listen. Theresa saved his eye after the last op, but the wound changed him."

Misha watched Michael pick up the headphones again, remembering the weight his son carried, though he gave no hint of it. Misha knew it well.

Christine came down the stairs carrying the dog. The tie that had bound her hair was gone. It would take extra effort to pass a comb through it, tangled as it was in asymmetrical tufts at the back and over one ear, smashed flat at the other. She didn't smile, but her light brown skin over prominent cheekbones glowed. Even the yellowing bruise beneath one sparkling eye seemed well on the way to healing. Any doubt Misha might have had was removed by Rimas's languid stride behind her as he approached the coffee machine.

Steve punched him lightly in the shoulder. Sergei looked up from the computer and grinned. Misha handed him an empty mug.

Rimas narrowed both eyes in confusion, bringing the edge of his scar into the vee formed on his brow. "How is this different from when I have been with Jade?"

"What do you mean?" Misha poured coffee into his mug, then into Rimas's.

"There is no such reaction by my friends when it is Jade."

"Perhaps because Jade does not smile so compellingly." Misha raised his cup toward Christine. She took a comb from Jade and headed for the bathroom, grinning. Fluffy followed her. "And also," continued Misha, "you are not usually as relaxed."

Rimas glowered. "You are hinting again that Jade is not for me."

"I am not hinting. I am saying it outright. This is proof. Pay attention."

"Christine is not for me, either."

He was implacable, defiant like Vasily.

"Perhaps not, but better a satisfying reality than a shadow fantasy. Vasily constructed a life he did not have, would never have, solely in his mind. As he came out of the hotel room where he bedded Gloria for the first time, we could see his intensity, his excitement. Not joy, not peace. It was more like how he approached placing charges to bring down a well-engineered bridge. I caught a glimpse of her standing behind him in the room, disheveled, troubled."

"That is not how I am with Jade, nor how she is."

"Not exactly, but two things are the same."

Rimas looked at his coffee; the furrow in his brow deepened, shielding his eyes, and waited.

"Like Vasily, you have constructed a lie and required yourself to believe it. Like Gloria, Jade complies. For Gloria, it was a duty. With Jade, a kindness. Neither is what you want."

"You are wrong. She loves me."

"Has she said it?"

After a deep breath, Rimas said with a hint of defiance, "Neither has Christine."

"I am not advising you to refuse what is offered. Only accept such boons without making up myths that will devastate you when shattered." Misha watched Rimas clear a look of momentary open rebellion from his face and continued. "Louis, Vasily, and I were waiting for the elevator when it opened. Darren Smith walked out of it and down the hall to Gloria's door. We knew who he was. His dossier was in Frank's file. It included a photo. He also knew us. Specifically, he knew Vasily."

"How?"

The return of curiosity was a good sign. Misha continued.

"Vasily was as well known in our world as his father had been. A rich target for any specialist wanting to be famous for bringing down a Sobieski. I saw Smith's reaction. It confirmed my suspicion about Gloria. Vasily did not see it—or did not wish to."

"Did she open her door to him?"

"No. Worse. He had a key."

"Then, Vasily must have believed you."

Misha shook his head. "He told himself a lie and saw only reasons to believe it."

"What about the op? Wasn't Smith your target? Wouldn't Vasily be glad to see him go?"

"Then, like now, we needed more. Our commission was for the entire network."

Misha poured more coffee into his cup. Rimas had let his go cold despite the heat of the room. The next question came in the form of an expectant silence, and Misha responded.

"Louis and I had difficulty getting Vasily into the elevator. He was the best fighter I have ever known, but we were more desperate. He was well bruised by the time we arrived on the ground floor."

"And his fantasy?"

"Lived on in his mind and nearly killed us all."

TWENTY-FOUR

Rimas wanted... he wanted... what the hell *did* he want? He watched Jade hit the print key, adding the printer's noise to the room as it surged into action, reams and reams of information they'd have to burn. No, they'd take it with them. If they lived. He wanted her, even with short hair. He would make her grow it long again. Christine was making coffee. What the fuck did she think she was doing wearing a ponytail in her line of work? So easy for criminals to grab her by the hair and....

He wanted Jade. But he wanted Christine again, too. Then again, mostly, he wanted to live.

The gun in his hand fit his long fingers precisely. He looked down at it and saw its history. Always history. From earliest childhood, his family impressed him with an appreciation of the past. The resistance against oppression. Mortal oppression. Deadly resistance. He rummaged in a footlocker for a cleaning kit and set it on the low table.

"I think I've earned the right to help."

Rimas looked up into Christine's dark eyes, the memory of her soft body still fresh. A response grew in his own body, whether responding to memory or anticipation, he could not tell. He glanced at Misha, who stood by the printer, reading from a thick stack of trac-tor-feed paper. Rimas made an executive decision.

"Sit down." He ejected the magazine and pointed it at an empty chair beside him. She sat. He turned the take-down lever and removed the slide. She unpacked the cleaning materials. They did not speak until he put the last piece on the table.

"I've never seen such a long spring," said Chris-tine. "What is that? It looks like a competition .22 or maybe a .32."

"It's a Modele' 1935. French. It fires a 7.65 French Long."

"It looks old."

"It was made before the war."

"Which war?"

He glowered at her, trying to stop liking her, trying not to let her like him.

"Okay. It's pretty old then," she said. "Is this the weapon that put the hole between that guy's eyes?"

"Why do you ask?" *Nosy.* Jade never pried like that. But then, she didn't have to.

"I'm a cop. I like to know when I discover a mur-der weapon."

Rimas scowled, not needing the uncomfortable reminder. "You know nothing."

"I surmise. Sometimes I get it right."

"You saw nothing."

"I walked through the crime scene."

"Alive. You walked out alive, yet I hear no grati-tude in your words."

She selected a bronze brush and screwed it into the end of a rod. She had picked the right caliber. Rimas could not help but be impressed.

"I would have thought my actions upstairs were a pretty big thank you."

"Your actions were to satisfy your own need. *You* should thank *me*."

He had to admit, but only to himself, that she was helpful, handing him what he needed as he cleaned each piece.

"You are a special kind of arrogant bastard, aren't you?" She held onto the patch she had been about to hand him. He snatched it from her fingers, grinning.

"You flatter me,' he said.

"So where'd you get the gun?"

"Misha—I mean Mack—gave it to me. It belonged to his friend, who was on the team."

"Is that the guy named Vasily he was talking about earlier?"

She handed him another patch. He shook his head as he took it.

"No. Louis. Mi... Mack says I am more taciturn than Louis, more like Vasily in manner, but he gave me Louis's gun. There are legends about him. He was very accurate."

"That's why Mack gave you his gun, then. You are also very accurate. I saw the hole in that forehead. Not even a double tap." She had become still and serious. Rimas was not sure why.

"One was enough," he said. "The weapon is very stable."

She spent a solemn minute watching his face as he worked.

"So why'd you leave the other guy alive?"

Rimas shrugged. What to tell her? "Charlie wants information."

"Funny way to get it, leaving him trussed like a turkey in a room with two dead guys. Skosh over there is having a conniption fit with Charlie. I suspect he disagrees."

"Skosh must arrange clean up with his local contact. He disagrees with the delay."

Christine leaned toward him. "Charlie's waiting for…?"

This time, Rimas knew precisely what to say. Nothing.

"I see. Or rather, I don't, but I know when I'm not supposed to. You guys do understand your trussed turkey's a helluva lot more dangerous than the fool I saw shoot a man in the park, don't you?"

Rimas found the silent treatment remarkably easy to do and repeated it. He figured she wasn't likely to hit him in the eye the way that filthy interrogator did.

She changed the subject. "Speaking of Skosh, I suspect there's some kind of triangle going on here, the way Jade looks at him.

He jerked his head up, chin forward, glanced toward the red-faced Skosh, sought Jade but did not find her, then glared down his nose at Christine.

"She does not look at him."

"You mean it's a surprise to you?" Christine squirted more solvent into the jar lid they were using for dipping patches. "I got the impression everybody was aware of it. Not healthy in a high-pressure environment. You know the old saying."

"What old saying?" Rimas did not move, could not move. He was reviewing a long list of smirks and glances, innuendos, elbows to the rib, quiet guffaws, a few winks, careful distancing, especially by Steve, in particular regarding Jade. Michael had made no effort this time, no arrangement for him and Jade. He was told it was impossible, yet he and Christine had not been impossible.

"What old saying?" he insisted.

Christine raised an eyebrow. "Don't shit where you eat. Of course, Skosh would have the same problem you have, wouldn't he?"

Rimas was silent again, but not by choice. The boiling in his gut showed itself on his face. The scar beside his eye ran a bright white warrior line down his flushed temple.

Christine screwed the lid on the solvent bottle tighter and glanced up at him. "I shouldn't have said anything. Don't tell me you're thinking about doing the whole fairytale fight over a girl thing. I can tell you there's no future in it. Some girls think it's romantic. but I'm here to tell you it's nuts. I speak from experience. My ex is doing life. He killed the love of my life in a fit of rage. Problem was, it wasn't just one life irretrievably damaged. Besides him, and me, and the guy he killed, we had a son."

Rimas noticed Misha watching him. Watching them. Reading the conversation. He breathed and dropped his chin. The woman next to him deftly threaded a patch into a slotted rod. She had remarkably graceful hands. And a heart-shaped face.

"But you are not for me either," he said to her.

"Never said I was. It doesn't mean I can't share what I have with you. A romp in the attic and a piece of advice."

"What advice?"

"A triangle will do more damage than one man with a Modele 1935. In a roomful of men with guns, it will be a catastrophe."

TWENTY-FIVE

"I didn't like the way Rimas stared at you at dinner, Skosh." Jade turned down the static on the radio attached to the center console of an old Ford that had spent too many winters in Quebec. Peeling best described its paint job. They had procured it from Rent-A-Jalopy. It smelled.

Skosh finished his dessert, a toffee chocolate bar, crumpled the wrapper, and threw it over his shoulder to the back seat. He didn't answer right away because he didn't know how to respond, how to tell her he knew a fight was coming on, and he intended to win it.

It occurred to him she might want some agency in this. It was almost the twenty-first century, after all.

"Yeah, I saw it, Jade. It was pretty belligerent. Did… um… did Christine mention…?"

"That she had sex with him upstairs? No. She didn't have to. Does anybody not know about it?"

Headlights in the dusk approached from behind their parked position. She read the plate as it passed. "Bingo," she said into the radio handset.

Skosh cleared his throat. Twice. "Does it…? Are you okay with it?" He held his breath.

"Okay? How? You mean jealous, heartbroken, insulted, devastated? I'm delighted. It's like finding a genuine Burberry trench coat in a thrift store for a buck

—which I've done, by the way. I couldn't be happier for them."

They let silence take over for a few minutes. Skosh used the time to wonder if she was using sarcasm. He decided she wasn't. He had to ask it."

"Why?"

She turned to look at him, saying nothing, punctuating it with a sigh.

He plunged. The most foolhardy moment of his life was at hand, and he went with it. The radio would explode with noise very shortly; this was his last opportunity, his only opportunity.

"Marry me."

"Don't go overboard on the romance here, Skosh. Is this an order?"

"Do you need an order?"

"I need more than two words.

"Okay. Please, marry me."

"You think it will work?"

"Frank does."

"Frank is managing my love life now?"

"So is Mack."

"Really? Mack?" The darkness hid her face, but the voice screeched a bit. "You think Mack will stop Rimas from killing you?"

"I can handle Rimas."

And he knew he could. Rimas was good, but Skosh was better, with more weight in his kicks to counter Rimas's agility. He could shoot almost as straight, and now that she said yes by not saying no, he had incentive. He had no doubt he would respond in kind if Rimas cheated by pulling a weapon. The specialists were right. No amount of meditation could erase the change in him from two years ago.

But he would not become one of them. He knew that now, too. The choice was his alone. He was in charge of how he spent his body. He did not have the long list of enemies the team had. Aside from Jade, there was no one in his life a would-be enemy could threaten. And he was perfectly capable of protecting her. His extended family would not interfere. They had disowned him long ago when he refused the marriage they had arranged for him.

The radio squawked. Mack was in their safehouse managing the network. Sergei had gone out with the others. The mic was picking up more than buzzing flies. He switched the audio to network.

Back to work.

Where the fuck are you, Paul?

A pause. It came over the Smiths' network and into the bugged room where Paul Smith lay bound and gagged in a swarm of flies.

Maybe we should stay away, boss.
The house is dark from this
side.

Dark here, too. Over.

Another pause.

I'm warning you, Paul. No games.

Then

```
I  hear  sourds,  boss.  Should  we
go in?

Wait til I get there.
```

"Yes, do," murmured Skosh.

"That's his license plate," Jade whispered as the car passed them, though their mic was off. They could monitor but not send.

Skosh picked up the car phone and spoke to it urgently. They settled to listen, with nothing more to do as the boss and two other men entered the unlit safehouse to rescue Paul Smith and slap him around for incompetence and bad luck. They heard him beg for water and waited in vain for the sound of a suppressor. The man was being allowed to live after he gave a complete account, including a pretty decent description of Rimas. He blanked on Mack and could only describe the crease in his summer wool trousers.

```
I  dunno,  I  dunno.  Shit,  give  me
some  water.  It's  been  hours.  I
heard  you  calling  but  couldn't
reach  the  radio.  Hours.  Fuck
these  flies.  Any  sign  of
Chatham?

He's  gone  deep.  No  sign  of  him.
I  put  out  signals,  but  he  hasn't
touched  them.  So,  you're  saying
it was the boyfriend?
```

Yes. Had to be. Fucking shot the
guy in that corner.

Who cut the other guy?

I dunno. I didn't see it. It was
so fast. They were out of here
too quick.

I know this mark.

The last voice was new, male, with no accent, but a hint of the foreign nonetheless. Skosh heard the careful language training in it. Knew who it must be. Of course. Leopards never changed their spots. If the aim was to disrupt, dismember, and destroy a functioning community, that guy had his orders. He'd pass them around to people like the Smiths. Plus, the man said he knew Mack's mark. This was an old enemy.

Frank called on the car phone. "Yeah, I know, Frank," said Skosh. "Keep the line clear. I need to call my Canadian friend as soon as they leave."

TWENTY-SIX

Chatham stumbled on a root, slammed his ribs against the trunk, a fir, and falling flat, lay still, listening. You never knew when one of them Serbs might be in the brush. He registered the smell of moldering needles and leaves. Last year's autumn feeding this year's green seedlings.

It was the comfort that warned him. Thirst was easy, brooks and puddles plentiful. Hunger came harder, but he recognized a few plants that hadn't killed him last time, and there were lots of slugs. He was careful about the fungi. Some of it was strange, but he avoided that and feasted on what he knew. But the comfort, the urge to close his eyes and settle into the dirt, to dream about home.... That was going to kill him.

He forced himself to stand. So they'd take him prisoner. So what? How bad could that be? Uncle Sam would ask for him back, right? Naw. There was no Uncle Sam for the white man anymore, Slava told him.

He swayed where he stood, left arm up high to hold a low branch for balance, squeezing his eyes tightly shut and then forcing them wide open. Where did that name come from? Slava. Rostislav. In the forest. Memory came in tiny parcels, like those little pepper packets they give you in an MRE to provide the illusion there would be flavor in your meal-ready-to-eat, and you were in control of how much.

He ripped open packet one. Slava was not in this forest.

Packet two. This forest was not in Bosnia.

Packet three. He again had to survive.

A low-frequency rumble caught his ear. He followed it and found transport, then drove it until he saw a sign pointing to a numbered road he knew would take him back to Montreal. He added power to the tractor, running it up and over an embankment, jumping out before it hit the water on the other side. He was sorry about that. Shooting the farmer hadn't been a problem, but the tractor was a good one. Even though he was white, the farmer talked that foreign stuff like the nigger in the park. Besides, he needed the guy's lunch pail, especially the sandwich.

Chatham climbed out of the drain and set out to cross a corner of the field. At the numbered road, he stuck out his thumb and trotted to the semi as it pulled over.

...

"Listen," said Yannick. "There's news."

Skosh regarded his counterpart as more than competent, a power-packed short man with quick manners and no time for nonsense, but his refusal to acknowledge Skosh's facility with the French language grated. "I heard your radio, Yannick. A dead farmer and a tractor. I got that much."

"And witnesses, including a truck driver."

"Yeah, I got that, too."

"What you didn't get was the gun he used was the same one that killed the man in the park."

Skosh scowled. They stood across from the blood on the living room floor of the other side of the duplex, watching the mop-up. Paul Smith and his boss had taken the radios. Yannick's clean-up crew had taken the bodies.

"So he's back in the city. Nice to know he's been away."

Yannick nodded, his smile sardonic. "The semi driver said he kept talking about a boss. He had to find this boss and tell him something. Stuff like that. The hitchhiker sounded scared and not too coherent, he said. The farmer was Quebecois. The driver is Anglophone. Maybe that's why he's alive. I told him not to pick up hitchhikers anymore for his safety.

...

Paul Smith ditched the pants he had peed himself in. The boss's safehouse in an economical hotel was not fancy unless, like Paul, you considered a working shower a luxury. His greying hair still damp and his clothes wrinkled but clean, he closed his suitcase and walked into the suite's living area to appear for sentencing.

The boss sat on a hard kitchen chair, facing the weird guy, who was comfortable in an upholstered armchair. Weird, Paul decided, because he was too calm, too quiet, and coming out of nowhere. Add the deference he received from the boss and the recipe called for caution. Paul was cautious.

"Paul, this is Rusty," said the boss.

He did not introduce Paul to the weird guy. That meant he had already briefed his life story to the man. Caution became more imperative.

"Hello." Paul kept his face under control and forced his muscles to relax.

"Rusty brings news." The boss's attempt at sounding optimistic produced the opposite effect. "Chatham is back in the city. He's looking for me. We believe if he thinks you're me and he finds you, then that'll kill two birds with one stone."

Which two birds?

"He's a lunatic, Boss, but way out of my league skill-wise. He'll shoot first. Somebody else will have to bag your second bird."

Both boss and stranger nodded slightly, impressed at Paul's grasp of how dispensable they saw him.

"Tell him Slava sent you," said Rusty. "He will pause to ask a question. Use it."

TWENTY-SEVEN

She would marry Skosh. Knowing it, just feeling the conviction, the understanding that Mack had ordained it, brought a different color to sunlight, a softness to shadow. It changed the nature of every task, every view, and all smells. Especially the smells.

Jade knew she had to give credit for better smells to the move back to their less crowded safehouse, but because it happened at nearly the same time as Skosh's proposal, it added to her new Elysium. She floated.

Then Mack walked into the kitchen.

They had a strange rapport, an uneasy way of relating to each other, like an uncle and niece in a fractured family. She was sure he considered her frivolous. She thought—no, she knew—him to be a violent man who filled the space around him with an almost palpable atmosphere of menace. She could not be easy around him but was somehow glad to see him. It had been two years.

"Coffee?" Jade surprised herself with her newfound ability to act normal in a situation that was anything but.

Only the barest lift of his chin indicated yes. She poured and placed the mug before him at the table as he took a seat.

Uncharacteristically, he spoke early. As she recalled, he usually waited until everyone around him was suitably uncomfortable.

"So you will marry Skosh," was his conversational opener.

"How did you know? Did you guys put a touch on that old beater of a car we were in?"

"You are calm and happy. There can be only one cause."

"It could be Rimas." She brought her mug to the table and sat across from him—like you could have a cozy domestic chat with this guy.

"Ah, yes. Rimas. You have yet to tell him. He may not take it well."

Jade swallowed coffee with a half choke. "How is the op going?" She wanted a change of subject.

He shrugged. "The target belongs to Charlie. My purpose here is not the same but is going well. Both plans, as always, may end in disaster, but we know much more now."

"So Christine's black eye was a big help?"

She tried an innocent tone, but he wasn't buying it. He raised his chin with a half smile and a glare.

"Yes. A huge help. We know who is using the Smiths, who leads them, and from what safehouse."

His use of the word 'using' meant they had traced at least one player to an intersection with another intelligence operation. Probably Russian, she thought offhand with a touch of pride in her newfound grasp of the game.

"How did you find the safehouse?"

"Paul Smith wears a scrap of tape on one shoe. I put it there when Rimas tied him. It will soon fall off and be discarded as trash, but the micro transponder it carries has already done its job. Sergei devised it. They unwisely chose a popular hotel of suites downtown."

"Why is it unwise?"

"It makes it simple to place a touch."

"But you don't like it. Why?" She wasn't sure why she knew. The man never seemed to change expression or tone. Maybe it was his easy acquiescence to her change of subject. He must want to talk about the op, she decided, even though it belonged to Charlie. *It bothers him.*

He did not exactly sigh. It was more of a puffy exhale but close enough. That and the extra time he took to speak again showed her the level of his concern.

"There are too many coincidences," he said slowly. "And too much is unknown. It increases pressure on the team."

"Surely the coincidence of Christine being here is a bit of serendipity, isn't it? It can work both ways."

"Yes." Another Mack-style sigh. "Her presence has been helpful. And it is always the case that no matter how carefully we plan, the situation will be fluid. In 1971, it felt the same. We barely survived it. Coincidence can be a trap contrived by an enemy. And now there is Yandarbin. Again."

"Who?"

"Anzor Yandarbin—an old enemy and capable of setting just such a trap. He will exploit any weakness. Back then, he worked mainly with the left. Our contract did not require us to gather intelligence on our quarry, only take them out. I had assumed the Smiths were also Marxists. It seems Yandarbin was not a slave to ideology even then.

"That's quite a shift. You know this guy?"

"In the killing game, there is very little space between left and right. Yes, I have met Yandarbin. He was KGB then."

Was that a wince? She caught herself worrying about him, told herself to stop it, and set aside the emotion to sort out later.

Frank came yawning through the kitchen door from the stairs yawning and headed for the coffee. "Did I hear you talking about old Rusty?" he asked as he grabbed a clean-ish mug and poured.

Mack nodded and explained to Jade, "Yandarbin uses Rostislav Tobrin as his game name; some call him Rusty or, sometimes, Slava."

Frank rubbed his prominent eyes under the yellow glare of a bare bulb hanging over the kitchen table and yawned again. "This is his op then," he said, "which means he knows we're here."

Jade studied Mack's face as the pieces fell into place for her. She liked Christine and hoped like hell she was not caught up with this new guy because if she was Yandarbin's tool, the solution would fall to Mack, and for the first time ever, Jade could read his expression. He didn't want to.

TWENTY-EIGHT

Paul Smith took a bite of the pastry before him, surveying the coffee shop, watching the door, and contemplating his next move. What move? He wondered. There were none left. The man he sought had killed in a public place on a busy street fully lit by the morning sun. Skulking in the corner of a dark coffee shop would not deter him. Paul waited for death to walk through the glass door at the front.

The coffee was gone, and still, death had not come. He would have to coax it.

A motel at the edge of town gave him a room at the back, away from the street, facing a wooded area. Chatham preferred wooded areas, shady approaches, and dark corners. Paul took the key from the counter and walked to his new, un-safehouse. He knew better than to think of it in any other way. Chatham would find him. He made sure of it by visiting the two nearest dead drops by day, never looking around, inviting a tail.

The mile walk from the drops to this dive helped Paul compose himself. He had long considered himself a dead man, accepting the ultimate consequence of his decision to serve the Lord in this way. The boss's offer of martyrdom should be grasped with glee, embraced as a boon, a guarantee of his membership in the elect. What was it then that niggled?

He pushed away the image of her face. He shouldn't even think of 'her,' only 'it.' It, then. A serpent's seedling with high cheekbones, dark hair, and a swollen lip. So inhuman, he reminded himself, that she did nothing when he hit her. It. Damn it.

It was that face, with those deep brown eyes, feigning intelligence, regarding him with understanding. That was it. A thing, a non-human, should not look through him. She never cried, spoke little, sounded intelligent. She regarded her enemy as being beneath her notice. He had seen it in her eyes.

For six hours, he had lain trussed like a steer at a rodeo, crying, shouting, suffering, and covered with flies. He peed himself. In all that time, the face peering at him from behind his lids each time he closed his eyes was not that of his blue-eyed savior on the wall calendar in his kitchen. No, not the Lord bringing vindication, but a calm, knowing gaze in a face that accused. It was the eyes—and the mind behind them. But she could not have a soul. *Could she?*

Morning rain dripped its last contribution to the day's summer heat, steaming the night's cooler air just enough to make it fresh. Sunlight broke through a hole in the clouds, pretty, hopeful, but the old motel before him allowed no touch of relief. He returned to despair and let himself into the secluded room at the back.

"Who the hell are you?" Paul discarded a brief notion of running. He recognized, of all things, the crease in those grey summer wool trousers and the Italian shoes, the last moving things before six hours in hell. The man sat in one of the stiff chairs on the other side of a small table—the one facing the door. Casually still, but ready to move.

"Call me Mack," he said.

"What the fuck do you want?"

"Information."

"Yeah, don't we all? What makes you think I'll give you any?"

Mack pointed to the other chair. "Sit down."

His back to the door, Paul accepted death a second time that day. This particular martyrdom was not going well. He understood nothing, trusted no one, and suspected it was all a bit pointless. He waited for the question before deciding whether to answer it, anticipating only the bullet that would follow, whether he answered or not.

Mack gave a minimal nod of approval as Paul placed his hands on the table. "Tell me about the woman," he said.

How did he know? Of all the plotting and danger and animosity Paul faced, how did this man know it was the woman that bothered him most? He tried to stop his face from betraying surprise—tried and failed.

Mack rewarded him with a half smile. "You once knew the woman who called herself Gloria Smith. She died in this city in 1971. Tell me about her."

Relief flooded through him. Paul did not bother to hide it, letting his memory spill out in words. "Her real name was Gloria Sessions. She had to keep the same first name when she went out to do God's work because she would always react to it. She was a little older than me, the daughter of a friend of my dad's. A real stunner. I was old enough to see that. Long blonde hair, grey eyes, a body any man would dream of. She wore hip-hugger bell-bottom jeans and no bra. I adored her. Most of us did."

"What happened to her?"

Paul shrugged. "She met a guy."

"In Montreal?"

"Yes, here in Montreal, too, but I'm talking about Stan back home in Colorado. He was a warrior for the Lord. We kids looked up to him. He was a great speaker, and we thought he was our champion. Gloria caught his eye. He took her under his wing, so to speak, and probably to his bed. She was maybe fifteen—sixteen? Nobody talked about that, but I don't see why he wouldn't have. He was quite a bit older than her, and I don't think her dad approved, but there was nothing he could do about it because she'd been tapped to do God's work."

"God's work?"

Paul nodded, warming to the subject, letting it strengthen his resolve. "To cleanse the planet of the serpent's seed, the descendants of Cain. Stan trained her to be a warrior."

"And he took her to Montreal?"

"Yeah. She'd do anything for him. The rest, I don't know. I was just a kid listening to the church elders talk while drinking brewskis out on the deck." Paul cradled his forehead in his hands, elbows on the table. He remembered those winter nights, all the men in their compound bundled against the cold, their breaths clouding the air. He hadn't understood it then, only caught part of the meaning now with the hindsight of adulthood. He picked up his head and met Mack's eyes.

"There was a name. And I heard it again recently. A funny name out of the history books. Charlemagne."

Mack only raised an eyebrow. Paul went on.

"And another name. It must have been her mission. Some guy named Vasily Sobieski. I'll never forget that. I heard it a lot that night. She was doing great and had him in the crosshairs, but something happened, and she came back to be buried. She was twenty years old." Paul let his glare convey a challenge, but he was careful to moderate it, trying to hold back martyrdom for a little while. "Did you kill her?"

Mack did not return glare for glare. "No." His expression softened with a momentary glance downward that returned to meet Paul's eyes. "Now, tell me about the other woman. What did you find in her pocket?"

Shit.

TWENTY-NINE

"You let him live?" Michael nearly choked on his sandwich, a bland concoction of lunchmeat and mayonnaise packed with protein and devoid of flavor. He made a mental note to tell Jade what he thought of the catering.

"You are surprised?" Misha curled a lip as he contemplated the stringy roast beef and stale bread he held in his hand. The dim light in the garage mercifully camouflaged the appearance of what they ate out of necessity.

"Of course, I am surprised. I have never known you to spare a cartridge on an enemy whose return round could doom the mission. Why, Papa?"

Michael took another bite of the sandwich, mashing it and not tasting it, concentrating instead on the other discomforts for a moment, the heat, fatigue, and worry, to get his mind off what his father had uncharacteristically done. Sweat poured into his right eye as he turned to glare at the man sitting in the car's passenger seat. This was the second time ever that he openly defied his father. The first had been his decision fifteen years before to join the team he now led.

Misha picked up the second half of his sandwich, looked at it in the dim garage light, and put it back in its wrapper. "Paul Smith may be more useful to you alive."

"How so?"

"Either he or Chatham will be eliminated, one by the other, without any agency on our part. If Chatham lives, he will be too disintegrated to be effective. If Paul survives, he may be turned."

"You think so?" Michael rested his chin on his knuckles, holding the top of the steering wheel. He saw his father nod out of the corner of his eye. "Why?"

"There is a tear in the fabric of his ideology."

"The ideology that killed my grandparents?"

Misha nodded. "I brought it into our discussion. He told me I was so obviously 'Aryan' I must be a race traitor and began explaining my eternal salvation and why the species must be cleansed of the contamination of Cain. It was all I could do to not shoot him immediately."

Michael looked at his father. There was no sign of emotion on his face or in his voice, but from long experience, he knew the words Misha had heard must have sparked a tempest of grief and anger. Michael envied his control. He waited, not needing to prompt.

Misha stared ahead through the windshield into the past. "I told him even I, an old assassin, do not believe the human species can be improved by wholesale murder. I asked why my brother, who was equally Aryan, had to be cleansed from the planet at the age of six. It must have been a mistake, he said. Only the soulless seeds of the serpent, those who are not white Europeans, particular races, he emphasized, who are not human, will be eliminated." Misha paused and turned to look at his son. "I reminded him that he has been nominated for elimination by his leadership."

"How did he react?"

"He stuttered and then fell back on the honor of martyrdom. What if, I asked, once his so-called martyrdom is accomplished, it turns out he is wrong and he is only an executed murderer of the innocent? He will be as dead as his victims. Perhaps they will be the elect and he, the damned."

Michael reluctantly took the last bite of his sandwich. His body needed protein for what was coming. He would be discussing this with Jade. He swallowed and met Misha's eyes.

"Did you tell him about Rusty? He has now met the man. Does he understand what he is?"

"That his salvation ideology is being used by a foreign intelligence service to disrupt his country? No. I did not have the opportunity. He changed the subject, pouring out his thoughts as if I were a confessor priest. He wanted only to talk about the woman."

"Which woman? The policewoman?"

Misha nodded. "I asked what he found in her pocket, and it sparked a long, emotional diatribe. He was in no condition to notice that we could only know he found something if we had been listening. By the way, have you taken up this mistake with Frank?"

"I did."

"What was his excuse?"

"He apologized and said he checked thoroughly for weapons but did not realize the little card in her pocket could be significant. Technology has left him behind. Then he thanked me for shoving him against a wall. Said it was like old times."

Misha smiled and shook his head. Michael continued.

"We have checked everything now, all her pockets and her shoes, and Sergei has been monitoring for outgoing signals all along, so barring new technology we are unfamiliar with, there has been no breach. I think if there were, we would have picked up on it by listening to them with our touch on their safehouse, as we did this lapse. I only wished they had said what, exactly, they found. What did Paul Smith tell you?"

"It was a ticket to Alcoa's speech." Misha pulled it from a pocket and handed it to his son.

Michael studied it, taking a moment to organize his thoughts, saying only, "That is concerning."

"Indeed."

"But she is not one of theirs?"

"She is not. She may be working for someone else, but he confirmed she is not working for the Smiths."

"How did he confirm that?"

"In his long, jumbled diatribe, I understood she is at the heart of his ideological disintegration. He questions everything because he cannot stop thinking about her."

Michael pushed his chin forward and raised his brows, allowing surprise to show itself. "How? What did he say? What were his words?"

Misha repeated the English words Paul Smith had used, the words that saved his life, at least for the moment.

"She has a soul."

THIRTY

Rimas was late for lunch. Michael had let him sleep for five hours. Why? The tub of food on the counter held a half dozen sandwiches, skimpy beef or fatty ham, thin mayo or rancid butter, wilted lettuce, or old tomato. He curled his lip and selected one of each.

He needed food. The bags of pretzels were the only saving grace of this meal. He needed salt as well.

He surveyed the room as he wrestled with gristle on stale bread. The babysitters had not yet come from the other house. The team would meet privately first. When Skosh and the others did arrive, Rimas would let Jade know what he thought of this lunch.

Misha, Michael, and Sergei stood together near the secure satellite phone. Steve sat in one of the uncomfortable chairs not far from them, a half-eaten portion of the sandwich in his hand. He was not chewing. He watched the three at the phone.

The room was too quiet. Only Sergei's face betrayed his emotion. Something was wrong, no doubt with Mara, and no doubt seriously—as in, deadly serious.

Rimas checked his watch. They had less than twenty-four hours to eliminate the targets, and they still did not know how many guns the Smiths planned to deploy at that speech. The wild card, Chatham, was still loose, outside the control even of the enemy. What a goat rope. He wondered about the expression, another of Steve's Texas idioms. He caught Steve's eye, raised one eyebrow as a question, and Steve left his chair to join him near the coffee machine.

"She's in labor," he said. "Seven weeks early."

Rimas wondered if any of the others felt the same combination of fear for what may become the loss of Mara and anger at her for choosing such an impossible course of action as to have a baby against medical advice. He moved one shoulder in an awkward half-shrug to hide his despair. "It is, as you say, a real goat rope."

Steve turned up one corner of his lips in a corresponding half-smile. "I'd say we've graduated to full-on cluster fuck, partner." He dropped the smile and continued before Rimas could pin down the definition. "You remember we heard Paul Smith find something in the cop's pocket but he didn't say what it was? We knew it wasn't a weapon; Frank is thorough."

Rimas nodded.

"Well, Misha asked the guy. It was a ticket. To the speech tomorrow."

Rimas inspected the ceiling then met Steve's gaze again. "She has been in the meetings. She knows our objective and said nothing."

"Precisely. Also, more news. Misha let Paul Smith live."

Rimas assured himself he hadn't formed a fantasy about Christine, but he liked her. Now, Paul Smith was an enemy still walking the planet after meeting with Misha. In ten minutes, small pieces of his world had tumbled around him, chunks of crumbling mortar raining down in warning that soon the bricks would follow. Jade's sudden failure at providing an edible lunch grew in consequence, not because it was important, but because it was another wrong thing.

Misha approached, limping and looking... old—a remarkable achievement for a specialist. Though his body retained most of its power, it was Misha's mind that mattered most to the team now, and, Rimas realized, especially to him. He needed strong mortar to shore up the bricks.

"Tell me more about Gloria," he said as he handed Misha a mug of hot coffee. He poured another for Steve.

"Gloria?" said Steve. "Who the hell is Gloria?"

"I have been telling Rimas about the operation here in winter 1971," said Misha.

"Oh, that. From the sound of it, that was also a real cluster fuck. I remember Louis talking about it. Everybody had a different agenda."

Misha nodded. "Rusty was here; Montreal remains his primary posting even today. His English is perfect, and he can pronounce the Canadian 'ou' sound, so he often passes as an Anglophone. He was then KGB, young but moving up. We discovered later that it was his idea to use the fascist Smiths to kill a Marxist nationalist who betrayed the FLQ extremists. At the time, only Frank suspected he was not a native English speaker. We could not hear it, but Frank insisted. It was the one element that helped us find the other threat besides Gloria and her lover."

"Lover?" Rimas arrested his mug before it reached his lips. "Darren was her lover?" He considered this. "Of course, the key to the hotel room."

"And the key to her behavior," said Misha. "On our second morning, the day after Vasily succeeded with her and we pulled him into the elevator, he went back to the coffee shop where they met. I made Frank go with him."

Misha set his empty mug on the counter and leaned more heavily on his cane. The move was subtle, the sole indicator of pain Rimas could see. "Frank never liked to be too close to Vasily. I don't know why. Without coercion, he did very little I required during the early days."

Rimas was acquainted with Misha's persuasive style. It explained Frank's persistent nervousness in his presence.

Misha continued. "Frank and Vasily entered the shop and found her there with two men. She introduced her lover as her brother, Darren, and the other man as his Canadian friend, Rusty.

"They had coffee and a pastry, and Frank heard the false note in Rusty's accent. He became more nervous than usual, Vasily told me later, which I thought must be something to see. Frank was jumpy most of the time back then, but perhaps it was an impression made by his prominent eyes. He pulled Vasily from the shop by his sleeve. One cannot say Frank lacks courage.

"Louis and I waited not far away, and Frank gave his opinion of this new man, Rusty, while still walking up to us. He is probably Francophone, argued Vasily. No, said Frank. He misused English articles twice. The French are all about articles, *le, la, les*; these are second nature to them. Rusty's first language doesn't use articles. It could be a Slavic language."

Misha looked significantly at his mug. Rimas took the hint, filled the cup, and waited. He shifted his weight again and went on with a sigh. Another dislodging brick in Rimas's world. Misha was definitely in pain.

"For a second time, we wrestled Vasily to stop him from strangling Frank." Misha smiled at the memory. "When our surveillance followed Rusty into the Soviet consulate, Vasily had to admit his precious Gloria was compromised, but he insisted she could not know it, was innocent, misled by her brother. The discovery put us on guard against our customary enemy but did not yet destroy Vasily's illusion about Gloria."

"Sergei says Rusty typically employs two back-ups," said Steve. "He's one of the few colleagues Sergei never cuckolded, probably because he was older and always in Canada. He heard about him in training."

Rimas recognized a significant puzzle piece falling into its place. "Then, do we have three against us?" That would be easy. Steve alone could take on three.

"Yes, said Misha, "but we know only two."

"But there is Chatham and Paul Smith and the man they call boss."

"Skosh and Jade are trying to identify this boss, but he is not the third specialist. He represents the American money behind the Smiths." Misha leaned lightly against the counter. Before Rimas could ask the obvious question, he answered it. "Skosh wants the funder; we want the killer."

"Similar to the time of Gloria and Vasily?"

Misha nodded minimally. "There are too many goals in too many factions, all of them armed."

Steve raised his mug to Rimas in a mock toast. "The very definition of a cluster fuck."

THIRTY-ONE

Fluffy made a racket, so Christine picked him up to quiet him. He always knew when change was imminent. Change made him nervous. Frank grumbled as he tried to tie a brown shoe with half a lace and a chewed eyelet. Skosh checked his H&K nine-millimeter before putting it in its holster. He picked up a handheld radio. Jade took a stack of papers from the printer and stowed them in a zippered pouch.

Christine edged backward toward the hall door of their safehouse, regretting the significant glance from Skosh that Fluffy's hysteria had called up. She had hoped to be forgotten. No such luck.

"You can let him do his business on our way over there," said Skosh.

"I will be okay here. It's secure enough and I don't mind the risk. I will keep an eye on things for you." *And use the phone, even though it's likely to be monitored.*

"No, my dear," said Frank. "You'll be wanted at this meeting."

"But I don't have any business attending your meetings, and I'd rather not know too much." *And I have people to contact.*

Frank gave up the struggle to make a bow and re-sorted to a knot to close his left shoe. "I agree it can be unhealthy, but Charlie particularly asked for you. He's not a man whose wishes we can ignore. Especially now. The speech is tomorrow. Even Yannick will be present via Skosh's radio."

There it was. Charlie knew. Of course, he did. Christine reviewed the past two days, searching for the threads he must have followed. No doubt Jade or Sergei or both had found every computer file in exis-tence with her name in it. They must know about her ex, about his sentence. Not many knew the rest, but Charlie was capable of too much thinking.

He stood by the computer with Sergei as she came through the back door of the team's house. Christine felt his attention, one hundred percent of it on her, and tried to veer toward the coffee machine on the counter.

Maybe he would forget, decide it wasn't necessary, ignore her.

The first thing she thought of, strangely enough, when he flipped the thin piece of cardboard between long fingers as he walked up to her, was how his hands resembled her son's.

"Do you play piano?" she blurted.

It arrested him. Why? Definitely a minimal hesitation in that still, controlled countenance of animosity.

"Let's talk about you," he said. "I'd like to go over your itinerary in Montreal. In detail."

"You mean my incarceration by you since day one? Or the beating I got when you abandoned me to the other set of criminals? What itinerary? I got here. I took the dog for a walk and witnessed a murder. Frank met me, said I was in danger, and took me to what I thought was his house. The rest, you know."

Shit. Belligerence? Really? I have to try it on with this guy? Where did that come from?

Now, everyone's attention focused on her. She heard a sudden quiet and felt the general tension in the air around her, especially those behind her, the babysitters and Jade. In front of her, she saw Steve Donovan's sardonic smile, Sergei's lip curled in a snarl. Rimas and Mack stood strategically positioned, with separation and sight lines preserved. Everybody looked as seedy as she felt despite the welcome change of clothes her suitcase had provided. Charlie's sleeves were rolled up, shirt collar open, shoulder holster gleaming, and weapon—a Glock—looking fully operational.

His slow smile made her swallow hard. The smile broadened, and she felt the blush rising in her cheeks. He raised his hand, holding up the ticket in those long fingers, giving her eyes an unwelcome focus point while her mind scrambled for a toe-hold on plausibility.

"It says 'Elder' under seating. Are you an elder?"

Stall for time to think. Come on, think.

"Where...?" She swallowed again. "How did you get that?" Memory blurred. She was sure it had been in her pocket. She remembered hands reaching into her clothes before and during that beating."

Shit. They're all in league. I'm dead. Alcoa has no chance. What were we thinking? The warriors were right. We cannot depend on the word of the White man for our safety.

...

Michael watched her think. Her face betrayed everything, pathetically easy to read. Every glance told him she knew her danger, and the blushes proved she was conscious of her mistakes, which were many. Point one in her favor.

But if she's not in the game, how the hell does she know about my music?

Point one against her. Even odds, so far. Maybe not —the music question was worth a thousand points against. She must have access to detailed intelligence. Police files do not provide this level of precision, do they?

The ticket, the lying, the coincidences. Points two to four against.

The dog. *Is he a point for or against?*

Fluffy strained in her arms, baring his teeth, riveted on Michael.

He decided the dog was a weapon, his weapon, and he would use it.

...

Christine's brain was unhelpful in coming up with an answer, but it excelled in observing, recording, and interpreting the next moment, rejecting telepathy as an explanation for the sudden move, but it was pretty damn close.

All Charlie did was point his chin in Steve's direction and crook an index finger in hers. No, not hers. Fluffy's. The dog managed a strangled yelp as Steve took him from her, clamped his muzzle shut, and locked his straining body into immobility until only his eyes could express his terror.

"He is innocent! Please! Don't!" She got no further than half a step before her arms were pinned behind her. When had Sergei moved? He was by the computer at the time of the yelp; she could swear it.

"Now," said Charlie, the voice low and smooth, his creepy stillness reaching new levels of malice. He raised the ticket again in those long fingers and manipulated it between them. To prove dexterity? "*You* are not innocent, are you? We will determine what you are before Fluffy dies of—shall we say—fright. I will have the truth from you."

Suspicion, confusion, desperation, she recognized the smell in the air because she was fully engulfed in it. There was just no safe way to explain, she thought, until she remembered the Mexican Mafia guy. They had him cold, but he had the information they needed. The DA cut a deal. For a reduction in the charge, he'd answer any questions with the truth. Every answer was brief and, indeed, true. They stopped the vehicle, found the compartment, and hauled in a high street-value load. Later, they learned five more truckloads made it through that night. They had never asked the man one key question: how many? He did three years of what should have been a twenty-year sentence.

The memory took no longer than Fluffy's yelp. Worth a try, learning from criminals. "Ask," she said. "I will answer. Truthfully."

Just not fully.

"So, is it to be a game of twenty questions, Christine? I am not playing. We have only hours. I must know what you are and why you are here. In detail. Begin now." He signaled Sergei, who released her arms but stayed uncomfortably close beside her.

"I came to hear Sydney Alcoa. He is an inspiration to us."

"You are not cooperating." He gave a significant glance in the direction of Steve and made sure she saw it.

"I am on his security team. I need to contact my deputies."

"You have deputies? Then, you lead this team you mention?"

Charlie raised his chin to someone behind her. Skosh stepped forward and scowled at her. "What team? There is no American team involved here other than the tangos."

Skosh might have thought his stern voice of officialdom would shake her. It had the opposite effect. She pushed her shoulders back and picked her head up. "There is a Native American team to coordinate security, and I lead it. I tell you this only because you say we have parallel objectives, and," she spoke through her teeth, "you have my dog."

134

"An ad hoc committee of volunteers can't do anything the governments—ours and the Canadians'—aren't already providing," growled Skosh, "but at least you're not armed. Stay out of this for your own safety."

Concern for my safety? Really? She closed one eye with a lopsided grimace of scorn. He had the decency to react. He threw his hands up at the absurdity of what he had just said and stepped away from her.

"Besides having to legally cross the border," she said, "I'm well aware of how the government views an armed Indian. We also know how much 'protection' we can depend on from the White man."

She was holding her own, keeping it short but not conceding. She could breathe. They would get out of this, she and Fluffy. There was hope.

Then, it was Mack who said, "Is it your plan to become armed?"

Too close. Hope wobbled. "No," she said, mentally crossing her fingers.

Charlie picked up the thread. "And your associates?"

She had argued against it and been overruled. He was waiting for an answer. It was taking her too long to grasp at one. She chose deflection. "We know we need not pull a trigger to be locked up for life by the White man's justice system." This was the most compelling argument that had won the day, the one she agreed with but argued against, the one that prevailed over her objection.

After four beats of no answer from her, Charlie said, "How many?"

Deflection. Deflection.

"We knew about Chatham. I was tailing him." *Ask me about that.*

"With a conspicuous dog? Really? How many?"

Fluffy whimpered.

"Two." *On my team.*

"Out of how many total on your team?"

"Three."

Mack chimed in again. The man had a dangerous mind. "And how many teams are there, all together?"

Shit.

THIRTY-TWO

When Michael gave them ten minutes to prepare for the meeting, Rimas set a chair next to the sofa where Misha sat sideways, leg stretched forward. Christine was directed to a chair across from him, between Sergei and Steve, where she sat hugging Fluffy, asleep on her lap. Steve asked her if she wanted coffee and she nodded.

Rimas stepped up to the counter after Steve, cutting in front of Skosh, grabbed two cups and brought them, full, back to his chair, handing one to Misha, then took his seat and watched the throng at the counter as he drank.

Two pots were soon empty. Jade started two more. Rimas saw her turn to Skosh, handing him a cup drawn from the bottom of the last pot. There was a fond smile. Too fond. Rimas would call it meaningful. Intimate? He could not see Skosh's face but could read the mutual pause in their body language. This was the first fully dislodged brick, falling from a great height of hopes and fantasies. It hit him in the solar plexus. He took a deep breath and turned to Misha, who was also watching Skosh and Jade—and, at the same time, him.

"Was this what Vasily saw?" Rimas asked in Lithuanian because he knew Misha appreciated the practice.

"*Taip*," said Misha. "He saw it on her face. We all saw it. At the coffee shop."

"Did he believe you then?"

Misha tilted his head a quarter inch, the closest he came to a shrug. "Vasily brooded. We went back to our safehouse and he would not speak—a new level of silence, even for him. We discussed who could be our third target. We knew only Darrell and Gloria, and because Rusty was involved, Louis and I argued there must be another. Vasily insisted there were two we needed to find because Gloria was not one. He left us, angry, saying he needed air.

"We trailed behind him, and once outside, he turned toward Gloria's hotel. We protested. Louis told him he was crazy. I tried to convince him to come back with us to our safehouse. He ducked into an alley and began to run. We ran after, of course, and climbed a high gate into a courtyard behind him, but by the time I landed on the other side, he had disappeared. Louis entered before me and thought he saw Vasily move left into a shadow. There were doors on both sides of the courtyard. All were closed, and there was only the sound of cats fighting behind us.

"Vasily was going to confront Gloria, we were sure, so we returned to the street and were coming off the elevator in her hotel when we heard the shot. Vasily had not bothered to suppress his Makarov."

Rimas considered. "He killed Darren."

"*Taip.* How did you know it was not her?" Misha drained his cup and handed it to him. The pots were full again.

Getting the refill saved Rimas from having to admit out loud that he wanted to kill Skosh. No doubt, Misha would disapprove. Wasn't the point of this story, or one of the points of it, that Vasily almost destroyed the operation? Was this how he did it?

As he poured, his eye rested on Christine, still hugging her dog. How vulnerable can you get? It must be why Michael let her live. Unarmed and emotional over a pet, any game she was playing must be strictly amateur.

There was nothing amateur about her lovemaking. It made him smile. She looked up at that moment and returned it, loosening the grip she had on that poor dog. He forgot about killing Skosh—momentarily.

...

Michael spoke carefully, monitoring Christine's reactions. Point two in her favor: he could read her every thought with ease. He sat across from her and began.

"Christine will now explain to us all why she is in Montreal, who the other members of her security team are, and what new complications we can expect."

She visibly composed herself with three deep breaths, loosening her grip on the dog, holding up her head, and sitting straight in that uncomfortable chair. Christine had made decisions.

"I have decided to accept your help in a limited way but will tell you only what you need to know."

Michael scowled. She damn well better produce what she had promised. He stared pointedly at Fluffy

138

to reimpose that leverage, though if she refused, he figured the dog would live, but she would not. He was fed up with her games.

"Proceed."

She relaxed at this acquiescence and began. "I am head of a team of three. You have been gracious enough to allow me to speak by phone to one of my deputies, John, to assure him again that I am okay after two days of imprisonment here, so you probably already know his full name anyway. The other is Eric.

"Sidney Alcoa is an inspiring speaker. He offers advice, hope, and leadership. Many people in the movement to secure our sovereignty and our rights will be present, primarily elders of the Eastern nations of Canada and the US, as well as a few who will travel from the West and Alaska.

"We know from history that we are not safe in our land. Some nations have begun to take a more organized approach to security, using training and techniques we have gained in the White world. As a police officer, I am naturally part of that movement, as are my deputies. John is a patrol officer in a small town. Eric works for Border Patrol. Both are from New England.

"What you want to know is how many are armed and how they will be deployed to protect this man. You also need to know something else, and I will get to that."

"Sometime soon would be advisable," said Michael. He saw her suppress a shudder. She would hold to the bargain, he decided, founded on mutual distrust the way any would-be alliance should begin.

"I am not armed," said Christine, "but my deputies are, and likewise, another team of three from a north-

139

western Canadian tribe out of the Yukon." She paused to suppress a smile. "They are all named Smith. An uncle with two nephews. Powerful fighters and armed."

"Smith," said Michael without expression, the irony apparent in the one word.

Christine nodded, her cheeks dimpling as she fought the smile. "The White man gave the family that name in the nineteenth century. It is not an alias for them. Or maybe it is a kind of alias because they have real names in their language, but most people can't pronounce them. So, they are genuine Smiths."

"Why are you the only person not armed?" asked Rimas.

Michael gave him an approving nod. The young fighter became more valuable by the hour. She took a moment to gather her words from where she thought they resided: on the floor, the ceiling, the coffee maker, the computer, and all points in between. Michael's patience, always tenuous, stretched to near breaking while her gaze bounced around the room.

"You know," she said, "or you should know the line between freedom fighter and terrorist is a river of mercury, with all crossings determined by the other side of the argument. I disagree with terrorism, but I value the right to self-defense. My own decision is more practical than philosophical. I like my job. I want to keep it. It is valuable to my people that I have access to the information it gives me.

"I told you we knew about Chatham, though not Paul or the man they call boss. It was you who introduced me to them." She glared at Michael before continuing. "Through my sources, we know about another threat. Four members of a gang of American skinheads have crossed the border, or will cross shortly, with a supply of weapons for a similar gang in Canada. I don't know how many are in that gang or how many will attend the speech. They will be equipped with ten assault rifles and fifteen semi-auto handguns, with high capacity magazines and a large supply of cartridges for all of it."

"How are they crossing the border?" asked Skosh, holding the radio to his ear. The question must have come from Yannick.

"By boat. Up the Richelieu from Lake Champlain. They launched from the New York side. I should say, not by boat, but by yacht. It's very comfortable, well equipped, and flying a Canadian flag."

"Who provided that to a gaggle of skinheads?"

Christine nodded. "I would also very much like to know."

"An important question for the governments, no doubt," said Misha, "but more immediate for us is how do *you* know about this gang?"

As usual, his father had seen the essential point, and Christine's face lost all color, confirming it as Michael raised an eyebrow. She lost more color, accurately reading his imperative in the small gesture. He was impressed.

She sighed. "We have a source in the gang." Confronted with only expectant silence, she went on. "He is a member of the tribe but looks very white. From contacts on that side of his family, he has become connected to several white supremacist groups." She paused again, almost choking on her next words. "He is very valuable to us and is the fifth man on that boat." She looked at each member of Charlemagne in turn. "I ask you to do what you can to preserve him."

It was in the wobble of her lower lip. This was too important to her. The rest of her information, whatever she was withholding, might not be essential to his team, but she had no business deciding that. Michael wanted the whole story, this piece included. Yet, she had come across with most of what they needed, largely in good faith, and if she was bona fide, their separate interests could blend well enough in this instance. His glance flew to Rimas.

Another weapon for extracting information from this woman. This time, she would likely enjoy it.

THIRTY-THREE

Fluffy growled.

"What are you doing here?" Christine asked as she shook off the torpor of a deep, replenishing sleep. "Hush, Fluffy."

"What do you think I am doing?" Rimas slipped his hands into her shorts with unerring accuracy. Her body responded as he reached the zone, but her mind demanded explanation.

"Charlie let you? Skosh let you?"

"Skosh does not dictate my actions."

Irritation marked his voice, and she remembered the triangle. *Fair enough, but that means…*

"So Charlie *sent* you."

His fingers became busier while the other hand cupped her breast. He covered her lips with his own, his tongue meeting hers in mutual exploration. Every nerve along the path of his touch fired a salvo of pleasure. *Not a time for discussion, except...* She broke off the kiss reluctantly.

"Slow down, cowboy. Let's make the most of this."

...

They emerged into the kitchen of an empty safehouse, a rare event on an op, Rimas told her. The coffee was still hot, and as he poured two mugs, he assured her somebody, probably Frank, would be monitoring all the sensors from the other house. He conversed with her, telling her about his brother, a musician in Lithuania. *Where the hell IS that?* She made a mental note to look it up later. If she had a later.

He asked polite, get-acquainted questions, sweetly, like he was interested. She gave him Fluffy's history. He asked about hers. She recited the good parts. He probed gently for the not-so-good, and she couldn't help it. She spilled some.

"Your ex-husband is in prison? For what crime?"

She nodded, swallowing hard. This was too close. "Murder." She croaked it.

He said nothing, only waited. It was not a word she wanted to leave hanging in the air, so she added some more.

"We weren't married anymore. There was... He was abusive and jealous." She took a deep breath. "He killed somebody I cared about."

"Was he also Native American?"

"Who?"

"Your ex-husband."

"No." This line of questioning helped. An oblique detour from the worst pain.

"Do you have children?"

143

Back to the bullseye.

"I have a son."

She said it without knowing how to put the rest into words. Everybody said Cody was a credit to her, but if Rimas asked how she felt, how would she describe the burden of fear? Her son was, after all, also his father's son.

"Does he look like you?"

It was almost a relief, another detour. "Oh, no, he's almost as blond as Charlie."

It was easy returning to the team's house because somebody—Sergei, according to Rimas—had thoughtfully cut a gap into the chain link fence at the back. They walked into a hushed kind of noise, full of movement and purpose, men dressing in black clothing, with protective vests and unobtrusive communication systems, slides chambering rounds, large capacity magazines loaded, H&K MP5 submachine guns going into hold-alls, Rimas had a murmured tête à tête with Charlie. Nobody else spoke. It was like a frenetic ballet of mimes.

There were tubs of food on the counter—if you could call it that. Something grey and congealed, evidently untouched. Another low-voiced discussion by Charlie, this time with Jade, who nodded quickly, face pale, and ran to the phone.

Rimas changed into the regulation black, slipped his Modelé 1935 into a holster on a web belt, extra magazines in Velcro loops on a black mesh vest over light-weight Kevlar. Now, that was a misnomer, thought Christine. There is no lightweight armor. Only two sizes, heavy and heavier.

An hour later, as Rimas piled into the SUV in the garage with the rest of the team, Mack led her to the Mercedes sedan and held the passenger door for her. "Where are we going?" she asked as he took his seat behind the wheel and pulled away from the safehouse. He didn't answer. Skosh and Jade were in the rusted beater ahead of them. Frank stayed behind in the team's house.

She was glad this time they didn't paint her face, attach her to that strange Russian, and use her to schlep heavy equipment, but having this particular criminal as a silent companion was no better. He made a left turn across Montreal traffic with no hurry, no g-force, and without hitting a pedestrian. At least he was a good driver. But he still didn't answer her as he headed east across the river, out of Montreal.

The silence continued until he turned the car south onto Autoroute 35 when she asked again. This time, he simply pointed to a sign giving the distance to St. Jean sur Richelieu.

"Are you taking me back to Vermont? I need to stay here, you know. My deputies need me to be present at that speech tomorrow. It's essential."

She stopped when he held up one hand, finger pointing to his ear. She noticed for the first time the earbud and wire he wore and answered his glance with a wry smile, wondering what he was hearing. The team, of course. They were somewhere ahead, as were Skosh and Jade. They meant business, for sure, and everyone traveled on empty stomachs with way too much firepower. Only Fluffy had said yes to a plate of whatever the grey stuff was. She rolled her eyes in protest to being kept in the dark, and Mack sighed.

He reached for the mic on his tie and turned it off, then flipped a switch on the main radio on the console. More silence, but with static.

She supposed she should feel flattered that he was letting her listen in. Then she heard a brief sentence in a low voice. In German.

Christine sat in the growing dark, listening to a language she didn't know for another half hour. Mack pulled off the highway and wound through residential neighborhoods as the sun sank into the flat earth to their right. She recognized Skosh's voice, but still speaking German. Experience told her these guys were about to pull a caper. All she could think about was Rimas in danger. That thought connected to Cody and then to despair.

Mack killed the headlights as they left the neighborhood and entered a waste area of broken-down heavy equipment and brush. He pushed that beautiful car through thorn bushes and over ruts until it rested only a foot or two from the gentle bank of a river. She saw the other bank as a dark line under a stars-only sky, unlit by a new moon. She figured it must be the Richelieu River, at a narrow point, maybe 900 feet. She knew because of the information she had given them. *They have additional intelligence they're not sharing with me and our teams. And, oh God—Cody. They are going to hit that boat.*

Skosh droned on, much good it did her, but she heard names. Mack's attention to it was total, and strangely, she felt the others listening through their earbuds from wherever they were on this river. Armed.

A voice interrupted Skosh, probably Charlie. Even the static paused, and in that short silence, Christine felt rather than heard a diesel engine. It grew into sound. She heard Steve's voice. "Secure." Unenlightening, but at least she understood the language.

Mack reached behind her seat and brought something to the front. She recognized a Gen 3 night binocular as he slipped it out of its case. An Omni V, quite new. He adjusted and watched as the dull throb of that engine grew nearer, but never louder, as it idled to the other shore. She saw only a patch of deeper darkness approaching and heard the engine cut before it stopped moving.

Mack turned on his mic and spoke, still in German. It sounded like numbers. He was counting. Charlie's voice came again, was acknowledged, then said something that broke off Mack's concentration and made him turn to her.

"You told Rimas your son is blond. These," he gestured across the river, "have shaved their heads." He handed her the binoculars. "Which one is Cody?"

Her hands shook as he helped her point and focus. She brought herself under control, concentrated, studied. Five green figures carried heavy boxes onto a small jetty. They all looked the same! Christine could eliminate the shortest, and that one was too heavy, with no grace in his movements. She studied the three remaining, all of them about the same height and weight. Nothing, nothing distinguished them. Nothing reminded her of the small tow-headed boy or the fine young man, the light of her life, until one of them pointed to a crate on the boat. It was the way his hand moved, the length of those fingers, glowing green in her vision, and she knew her son.

"He's the one on the jetty, farthest from the boat."
Oh God, let me be right.

Mack spoke to his mic. As she watched, she saw them fall, saw the heat from the muzzles around them, but heard very little. All was suppressed in a pantomime of death. The one on the jetty, farthest from the boat, remained standing for only a moment until another figure appeared from his right with astonishing speed and bore him down.

"Your name," said a heavily accented voice in English. She recognized Sergei.

"I'm not telling you nothing, mother fucker."

The sound of Cody's voice flooded her with relief—and tears. Mack pressed his mic and made a suggestion in German. She exhaled and lowered her head to clear her vision, then watched again as another figure approached the two on the boards of the jetty, and she heard that slow Texas drawl.

"So tell us, Cody, all about the animal your mother is willing to die for."

The figure pinned under Sergei became still, then replied, "Are you talking about Fluffy?"

THIRTY-FOUR

Euphoria had worn off. Jade still had to break up with Rimas and tell him about the engagement, and at the moment, all she wanted was sleep. And privacy. And Charlie was right, damn him, decent food. She sat at the wheel of the babysitters' car, parked a few feet from the aftermath of mayhem. At least she didn't have to watch somebody she loved being beaten and trussed. At each gasp, she glanced at Christine in the passenger seat.

"Did Mack explain before he dropped you here, Christine? This is just to make it look good in case anybody's watching. Yannick's people are beyond those trees with one of the guys who was taking delivery of all that hardware. The other one's dead. I assure you, Steve and Sergei are pulling their punches."

The darkness inside the car obscured Christine's face, but her breathing was readable. She exhaled. "Does Mack ever tell anybody anything? I wouldn't mind if Cody was blown enough to make those skinheads kick him out. I want him to quit this. It's a boulder sitting on my chest, and I can't shift it."

In the past two years, Jade had begun to understand a few things. First, her more trusted status with Mack. He told her more than he did most people. But besides that, repeated encounters with this team gave her a glimpse into the nature of having enemies. "Christine, Cody can't quit this if he leaves behind a bunch of reasons for people to want him dead. The team is trying to give him a way out. Do you think he'll take it?"

Christine took a full minute to answer. "He is his father's son as well as mine." After another pause, she said, "Except he's not heartless. We have disagreements."

Jade waited a beat or two, then prompted, "About?"

"About the best way to retrieve our rights, for one. And about his future, of course. He is just under half Abenaki—I had a white great-grandparent, and maybe one further back—but you wouldn't know it to look at him. There are so many things he didn't face as a kid. Teachers never discounted him. Nobody ever ignored or sidelined him or—It's hard to explain to somebody who isn't considered... less than."

Sergei hoisted Cody to his feet and frog-marched him to the SUV as it pulled closer to the jetty. Jade pulled the old car onto the road and headed for the bridge to Montreal. "I grew up 'less than' in my family," she said. "Nothing I did was ever good enough. I can't imagine what it would be like to face it everywhere. It would even be hard to just be anonymous."

"Exactly. Cody has an advantage, but he let his father introduce him to these men he met in prison. Political, violent gangsters who hate everybody. So, instead of working on his music, my son decides to use his whiteness to gain information and access to one of the gangs. He is twenty-two. He should be finishing his degree!" Christine stopped, sighed, and in a near whisper said, "And it's so fucking dangerous."

Jade heard the confused mix of emotions in Christine's words and the way she spoke them, sometimes breathless, occasionally choking. She was the mother of a child, after all, worried for but proud of the adult, scared to death of the fate he seemed to be choosing. Jade looked forward to children, Skosh's children. Her only concern until now had been to hurry up and get started.

This conversation brought new questions. She was pretty sure none of the team, whose lives were frankly shit, had a mother still living, but she thought of Sergei's wife, also a vital member of the team, instead risking her life to give birth to a son. She knew she would do the same. But all these guys were white, and presumably, if they wore the right clothes and behaved themselves in a certain way, they blended, became invisible, at least in most parts of the world they inhabited. Skosh's child might not. Were people really that narrow? She remembered hearing the Smiths on Sergei's tapes talking to and about Christine and the disgusting language they used.

"Of all the hazards a child faces growing up, I can't imagine that one, Christine. I'm sorry."

"I think every parent wants their children to do better than they did," said Christine. She brought her hands up before her face, fingers spread wide, shaking. "But Cody is so talented! He doesn't have all these barriers, and he chooses this?"

Layer after layer of realization struck Jade as she turned the wheel and accelerated onto the bridge. She had read all of The Section's files on Charlemagne, which weren't many because of their policy of breaking into her system to erase. Way back in the day, as a youth, Charlie had attended a prestigious European conservatory. How did they manage the security? She wondered. And after all that trouble so he could study, Charlie chose this? What did Mack think about that decision?

...

Mack turned the radio knob, changing it from Jade and Christine back to the network the team was using to dry-clean their way back. Skosh sat in the passenger seat of the sedan, staring ahead, still processing the fact that the bastards had bugged the babysitters' car. *Of course they would. Why not?* Then he turned his attention to the conversation he had heard, glancing at Mack behind the wheel, who stared straight ahead into the gloom, frowning. Skosh mirrored the frown, and they waited in silence for Yannick to come clean up the mess.

THIRTY-FIVE

They sat on the basement floor of the team's safehouse, enjoying its cool temperature. Skosh tried not to think of the eight-legged co-inhabitants lurking outside the glare of fluorescent shop lights hanging from the floor joists above them. He distracted himself from the thought by wondering if Jade would object to their children having Japanese middle names. It might be a sop to the extended family, an amendment to their perpetual disappointment in him.

He studied the face of the prisoner and decided the bruises were not all that bad, considering. The angry snarl was not justified. Mack had taken a high stool over by a work table under the stairs. Sergei stood at the last step down, MP5 casually pointed in the direction of Christine's angry son. He was steady as a rock. Considering the strain of no news since the bad news about Mara, Skosh was impressed. The man had righted himself somehow, or adrenaline had kicked in, and he was now himself, or at least, his operational self. Meaning focused and deadly.

Charlie held court, Steve on his right, Rimas to his left, at the top of a circle surrounding Cody, defined by Mack and Sergei at the bottom. Christine sat across from Skosh, to the left of Rimas, Fluffy in her lap. The cool, dusty floor underneath him made Skosh wish he could sleep down there. But then, there were the spiders. He shook off the image and marveled at Mack next to him. Even without the benefit of the cool floor, the man looked as comfortable as ever. He always did, no matter the ambient temperature or the state of his left hip, injured earlier in the decade. Skosh closed his eyes at that memory.

Charlie got on with it.

"Before we arrange for your escape, Cody, I need information, and you're going to provide it."

"I don't know who the fuck you are, man. You won't get nothing from me." It was a remarkably deep snarl from someone so young.

"Call me Charlie."

It was said with the usual cool, low voice that could still make Skosh miss a breath, only the lips moving with no other facial expression. It wasn't the cold basement that made him shiver. This was his job, Charlie included. He hoped the bald rookie in the center of the circle had the sense to step carefully.

Cody's Mama intervened. "Cody, this man is an ally. Please cooperate." There was an emphasis on please, complete with clenched jaw.

"He's a creep, Ma."

"I know, but there's more going on here."

"Those guys are dead, Ma. Fucking dropped where they stood. All around me. I mean, what the fuck? They were shit, but it's pitch dark, and suddenly, boom. I dunno what happened to the Quebec guys. There were two when we got there."

"Cody, listen to me." Finally, she turned on her mom voice, leaning over her folded legs toward her son. "There is no time to process all of it. You have to answer Charlie's questions. Now. The speech is tomorrow—later today. Everybody is dealing with developments. We are, and these guys are, and like I said, these guys are allies." She slowed to add emphasis. "Not very nice ones. Do you get my drift?"

"I get it that they've taken you in. Grow a spine, Ma."

Skosh wanted to slap the puppy but instead added his own few words with forced patience. "Your mom didn't have a choice, Cody. I'd say she did pretty fucking well in the circumstance, and you being alive is proof."

"I was about to meet a bunch of Canadian skinheads, asshole. Now I'm blown."

Charlie rolled his eyes up and over into a side glance, eyebrow raised, toward Skosh. It was a signal giving him charge of Cody's education. Again, he resisted the urge to use Charlie's usual methods, electing instead to continue with uncharacteristic patience.

"Get this through your thick skull, fuckhead. We've gone to great lengths to make sure you're both alive and not blown. Those two Canadians you're worried about, well, one is permanently not an issue. The other is being held by the Mounties. He'll have some legal troubles and be released to tell his friends that one of the Americans on that boat was beat up pretty bad and taken prisoner.

"For now, you're out of this op. You can't show your face anywhere until after the speech. That's when you'll escape, and if you're not a total pain in the ass, we'll help you cross the border and maybe give you a sandwich to tide you over till you reach civilization." Skosh ended with a grimace at the thought of one of those sandwiches. Justice comes in many guises.

But defiance and anger remained features on Cody's face, contorting his lips in a sneer. "I'll die before I..."

This called for more mother's wisdom, and Christine gratified Skosh, and probably the others, by jumping right in.

She tilted her head toward Sergei by the stairs with the MP5 pointed at her son. "Baby, when that guy had you on the ground, and somebody else asked you who I'm willing to die for, you said Fluffy, but really, the only one I'd die for is you, Cody. What I'm willing to do for Fluffy is go on living. He has no one else. Please accept reality and go on living. For me."

Fluffy lifted his big ears toward the prisoner, bared his teeth, and set up a low growl.

It was the only sound in that basement for almost a minute while Cody watched a tear escape down his mother's cheek. He turned to Charlie.

"What do you want to know?"

THIRTY-SIX

The heat hit them and then climbed higher. Michael wished they could have stayed in the cellar, but there was no telling how many tunnels of sound might be at work in this safehouse. He needed his father's advice and a secure way to get it. They sat in the sedan in the garage, boiling. An observer would think they did not show it, but Michael was sure they both felt it. He knew he did.

"This problem is not entirely the same as it was in 1971," said Misha. He sat on the passenger side with the seat reclined slightly, no doubt to ease his hip.

"How is it the same?" Michael considered this the first question.

"It is the same because we know Yandarbin. It is different because we did not know him then. We learned quickly. He has been consistent through the years, according to the intelligence. We did know at the time that he was using a third asset, but we did not know who."

"Then that is similar, Papa. How did you learn there was a third?"

"From the primary source of all intelligence. Pillow talk. Gloria let it slip the first time she was with Vasily. She said a name."

"I thought he resisted the idea she was in the game."

"He did. But he remembered the conversation when he briefly conceded she might be dirty after she introduced him to Rusty. She had mentioned a man named Antoine. He said she spoke the name with awe, and it bothered him. An important person, she told him. She could not wait to meet him."

"What was the context?"

"That she expected to see him in Montreal."

"Another Smith?"

Misha shook his head. "No. Not one of her group. Vasily was clear about that."

"Then all you had was a given name? Nothing else? We don't even have that. Is that the main differ- ence?" Michael wanted to start the car to use the air conditioner, but carbon monoxide was as deadly as he was.

With another shake of his head, Misha continued. "The difference is that you know more than we did. We knew nothing yet about Rusty besides his employer and only recently had encountered the phenomenon of the sleeper agent. A few weeks before Montreal, we had met our first one. It was another disaster for Vasily. Because of his name, he was much sought after by our enemies at the time."

Michael held the wheel with both hands at the top and lowered his forehead onto his knuckles. It only increased the heat. He took his father's example, sat back, and reclined the seat a little more. It helped. "Are you saying we are looking for a sleeper?"

Misha dropped his chin minimally in a kind of nod. "You know there are no other specialists here. We are hours from the event; the Canadians have good watchers. We have access to all of Jade's files, though she does not know it, and Skosh assures us his counterpart Yannick reports no known operatives in the area. Besides us."

Michael stretched his neck, looking at the ceiling to take in air. "I am aware, Papa, that Cody's band of skinheads and their Quebec friends are beneath Yandarbin's notice. I get that. So now you are saying there is someone already in place, someone close, who has Rusty's remit."

"Precisely. It was the Smiths who deployed their skinhead fellow travelers. Rusty has more finesse. In the weeks before the 1971 op, we were in Florida. Vasily met a girl he liked. She died from a bullet meant for him. The shooter was a sleeper."

"Was the shooter the one you were after? What was the op itself?"

"Frank's people had information the KGB had turned a deep cover mole, not yet activated. His office devised a way to use us to bring him out of the cold. They lied to us about the op and hired us knowing Vasily's famous name would give the enemy an incentive to deploy their sleeper. There were still many in the KGB who remembered Vasily's father. We knew the Americans were lying but took the commission because we needed the intelligence it would get us."

"And the mole acted?"

Misha looked out the side window into the past. "Yes. Vasily's infatuation with American girls was becoming a habit. When this one moved into the line of fire meant for him, Vasily could not save her. He did not speak for days after."

"You would be a high-value target, Papa, and Rusty knows your mark. He knows you are here."

"But initially, he could not know Charlemagne would be engaged for this, nor that I would be here. Everyone is aware I have retired. It is an unheard-of thing and therefore, famous. And here I am, unexpectedly. Rusty does not control Alex. Nobody does, including me. Similarities and coincidences go only so far, remember, but you can make use of them when they occur. As he will."

They sat in sweating silence while Michael reviewed similarities and differences, especially differences. He began with, "The Americans have not set us up this time."

"Correct."

"The purpose of Rusty's second backup is to kill Alcoa if the Smiths fail."

"Which they will."

Misha nodded. "The purpose of Antoine was the same. Vasily's presence was serendipitous for Rusty. A similarity."

Misha again agreed.

"You were seeking two; one was dead thanks to Vasily, and the other was Gloria, and Antoine was only a name. We don't even have that."

"But you have a deep understanding of how sleepers are made, Michael, and where they are placed. Use that." Misha paused, turned his head to look at his son, and gave a quiet order. "Use everything you have."

Michael sat forward, dropping his forehead onto the wheel. Sweat poured down the back of his neck and under the shirt collar.

"If anything happens to you, Papa, Alex will kill me."

"I am ancient history in this business, Michael, far exceeding life expectancy already. And like Mara, I make my own choices. Alex knows it. She also knows every one of us, my new grandson included, if he lives, depends on the team for safety. Charlemagne must not fail. The predators will not hesitate to destroy us."

...

"Who solved it?" asked Michael as he came down the stairs well before dawn, fresh from a two-hour nap. He felt the temperature change on the sixth step.

"Skosh," said Steve, stifling a yawn.

Michael surveyed his domain, his command post, his GHQ. Sergei slept at the computer, head nestled in his arms. The screen played a new saver, black and red monsters with fangs. Sergei was feeling savage.

Better savage than suicidal.

Rimas leaned back under a waterfall picture, his chair propped against the wall on its two back legs. Michael's father had stretched out on the sofa, an arm over his eyes. The coffee machine steamed. Skosh sat near it in Michael's stuffed easy chair but left it fast as he stepped off the staircase.

An air conditioner stuck in the darkened front window provided the only noise—and copious amounts of cool air.

"It took you long enough, Skosh," Michael said as he headed for coffee.

"Wasn't me. Jade bought it. Sergei installed it."

Michael knew he should be gratified. The two unreliables, one in each camp, team and babysitters, had somehow righted themselves. Jade was doing her job again. Sergei had adopted a more grim version of his ultra-competent self.

If he could be sure they were not about to face an entire army of sleepers, or if he could have any idea what Rusty was up to at that moment, Michael would be more confident. The swirl of contradictions and volume of conflicting intelligence pushed him to a decision. He woke his father, briefed him on what he meant to do, and signaled to Steve to change into a suit. They left during this quiet time, everybody in the same room, stealing uncomfortable patches of sleep while technically on watch. His father would pick up the threads if this did not go well.

THIRTY-SEVEN

Paul Smith remembered a name. Strangely enough, it was his own. Damon. They called him Damon when he was a child. His father was Mr. Kowalski. Mack's visit brought it to mind. The young Damon Kowalski became a warrior, a martyr in waiting, as he dropped his handful of dirt onto Gloria's casket when her body came back to Colorado from Montreal, though he didn't even know her—at least not to speak to. From that day, he dedicated himself to destroying the soulless sons of Cain. He joined the Smiths the next year and took the name Paul. Fought the good fight, killing in the name of the Lord, learning to conspire in the catacombs.

It was fucking hot in this motel room. He left the door open to air it out. To speed the attack, he sat facing the door in the dark, propped against the bed pillows, his Luger in his hand under the covers, next to his thigh. *For God's sake, Chatham, you need a fucking engraved invitation?* The night sky over Montreal was light enough to show a silhouette. It was all he would need. He'd blast anything that moved.

At midnight, the heat drove him outside for air. Stumbling through the trees at the edge of the parking lot, he pushed away the intruding dark eyes peering into his mind, the profound humanness in her expression, the challenge of her contempt. Each slap he'd landed on that face raised a bruise on his conscience. Tree branches stung his face as he pushed his way through them in a fruitless circle, counting the bruises, his, hers, and others. All the others. Would they matter in the reckoning? Would they keep him out of the elect like Mack said? He decided he'd rather not die this way, in thrashing ignorance, and broke out of the little wood near his car. He drove it back to the boss's safehouse.

Off the elevator and to the left down a long hallway, he passed a stairwell, then a man heading into the stairwell. Suit and tie. *In this heat?* Biceps, blond hair, the look that made the skin on the back of his neck tingle.

Paul still had a card key to the suite door in his pocket. He approached slowly. The boss was good at giving orders but knew nothing about security. He let himself in without knocking, his Luger in his hand at his side, not sure if he would use it or on whom. The boss was a candidate. To turn the light on, you had to slip the key into a slot beside the door, but he didn't need to. He could see plenty from the street lights below the open window. And he could smell it. He knew that odor well, having spent six hours immobilized next to a large pool of it.

He touched nothing. Kept his shoes out of it. Only checked how many. Two—the boss and somebody he didn't know. One by the window, one in the bathroom. The room had been tossed. The boss's pockets emptied.

He tiptoed out and closed the door. He would park someplace busy and sleep in the car.

. . .

Chatham watched the motel from a sheltering shadow on the edge of the wood as the man who must be the boss crashed into the open like he was being chased by a ghost. He wanted to talk to him and ask forgiveness but thought better of it when he spotted the room with an open door. Sure enough, it was empty. There was half a pizza on the little table. Chatham barricaded the door with a moveable dresser, ate the pizza, stood under the shower for twenty minutes, and slept—with sheets and pillows—until dawn.

...

Eric and John finished their walk around the park where Alcoa was to speak the next day, or rather later today since it was after midnight.

"Do you think she'll be here tomorrow?" Eric asked, his right eye winking fast in a kind of twitch, as it always did when he was nervous. He played his flashlight across the top of a high retaining berm surrounding the seating area.

"I'm not sure," said John, hearing Eric's nervousness but not seeing the twitch in the dark. "She was pretty rushed. Something about another team, and she couldn't get away. She acted like she couldn't speak plainly. I wish you had taken the call. You might've been able to tease more out of her. She likes you. She said the dog is okay. I was worried about it after she disappeared. When I watched her interview on TV, I figured the dog being shown like that could lead the killer straight to her."

"Did she say anything about what happened?" said Eric. "She should be armed. You would think a cop would know that. You're a cop and you're armed. I mean, it's part of the uniform. I don't go anywhere without my Glock."

"That whole uniform thing might be why she doesn't want to be armed here. On the TV news, she looked ordinary, in shorts and a T-shirt. Didn't look bad either."

Eric turned off his flashlight. "Doesn't she have a kid? Somebody said she was married to a white guy."

"I don't know anything about that. She's pretty private. Except for the dog. Fierce little thing."

"I have no use for unarmed cops."

"She says she's only here to supervise, and she's going to be right up close to Alcoa. No mistakes, no Rambo disasters is her mantra. Don't know if I agree, but I respect it. And I like her." John hoped Eric would hear the irritation in his last sentence and stop trying to goad him.

"Rambo? You think she was talking about me?"

"Maybe."

They walked back to the hotel in silence. When they got to the room, John took a long shower to help himself relax and sleep the few hours left in the night. Eric had gone out by the time he finished. Probably taking a walk for the same reason, he figured, to calm down. The guy needed to. He climbed into his bed, turned out the bedside lamp, and fell immediately into an untroubled sleep, waking to find Eric's bed still made.

THIRTY-EIGHT

Skosh reclaimed the comfortable chair when Charlie and Steve left. No sense in letting it go to waste. He considered the watch rotation in the other safehouse. Who would be up now? Frank, he decided. He briefly contemplated a quick sneak back to the sleeping Jade until he noticed Mack's blue eyes on him. *The bastard's reading my mind again.* He practiced three emptying breaths and saw Mack's recognition of that, too.

Rimas leaned against the wall to his left, chair and all, chin up, mouth open, eyes closed. Mack poked his midsection with his cane. The young fighter reacted predictably, pulling the Modelé from under his arm, but Mack was ready, using the stick to force his hand and arm up and to the outside, a trajectory that would put a bullet into a stair tread, nothing more. But Rimas was just as quick, awake before the barrel left his holster, aware before his finger entered the trigger guard, recognizing Mack before the f-word left his throat.

Mack took the stiff-backed wooden chair Skosh had abandoned and raised an eyebrow at Rimas, who took the hint and went to the coffee machine. He came back with two mugs and handed one to his boss. Skosh had become comfortably invisible.

Except for the droning air conditioner, the room was quiet. Sergei slept soundly on his keyboard. The only light was near the back door, giving the corner where Skosh sat a private, confidential mood. He practiced the stillness he had been learning in the presence of a world master of that skill.

"What do you want to know, Rimas?" asked Mack, as usual, reading the young man's mind.

Rimas moved his dark blue eyes, black in this light, up and away in a minimal shrug, thought better of it, and said, "What happened, of course? I want to know what happened to Gloria. Did Vasily kill her?"

"Not yet." Mack dropped that two-word foreshadow of his story's end in the dim, silent room, where it sat on the bare floor between them, presaging near-future explanations of long-ago pain. Skosh and Rimas waited, Skosh without breath, Rimas without expression. Mack resumed. His voice seemed to come out of the gloom itself.

"We caught up to Vasily at Gloria's new hotel on Rue de Guy. He came out of her room as we reached the floor. We took the stairs this time, having no time to wait for an elevator. He greeted us smiling." Mack allowed himself a huff of exasperation. "She was innocent, he insisted. Grieving for her brother. It had all been a terrible mistake, and he should have waited for verification. He did not tell her he killed Darren."

"What did you do?"

Mack's answer was interrupted when the back door opened. Rimas reached into his holster until Christine stepped in. Fluffy followed.

"Frank does not make good coffee," she said.

"He never did," said Mack.

She took a cup from the countertop, checked it for reasonable cleanliness, and poured, then stood near Skosh, drawing, he thought, unwanted attention in his direction.

"Find a chair and bring it here," said Mack. "Do not stand over us. We are discussing the past. I now have more of it than I have of the future, so I like to share."

Skosh relaxed when Christine settled near Rimas, shifting the weight of Mack's audience away from him. Fluffy jumped onto her lap, and Mack gave her a summary in English before resuming.

"Louis wanted to argue with Vasily. I told him to stop pressing and gave a little shove when he persisted." Mack paused and smiled slightly at the memory. "Perhaps more than a little shove. We covered each other to the safehouse. Vasily's movements were animated, free, happy—rare in him. Louis stomped. I spent the time worried.

"Frank's assistant met us with dinner. I needed a rational discussion about Rusty's backup, Antoine, but though the assistant had the clearances required by Frank's office, I did not want more ears hearing our disagreements. Frank has always been careless about files."

Mack gazed pointedly at Skosh, holding it there long enough for Skosh's studied stillness to crack and betray discomfort by shifting his weight. Skosh got the message and Mack continued.

"We were already disrupting ourselves and did not need additional help from the enemy. The assistant felt my stare and correctly decided to leave. He was using the name Harry Sycamore as his game name on his trip."

So, they had already compromised our files way back then. Skosh presumed that as a cop, Christine understood the many uses of information. He watched her expression. She was as adept at controlling it as he was trying to be.

"When Harry was gone," continued Mack, "I signaled Louis to check for devices and suggested Vasily should get some sleep. He was reluctant, with the blank, obstinate expression I had known since our childhood. He stayed awake in an angry turmoil over Gloria."

Skosh wondered if the grimace came from the memory or the present-day pain in his hip. Mack continued.

"Louis found a device behind a wall clock. It could have been placed at any time, but it meant our safe-house was blown, so we moved to a hotel on Rene Levesque Boulevard. The street was called Dorchester then. Vasily's anger cooled with activity, and we were able to discuss a plan.

"The FLQ informant the Smiths were targeting was to see a magistrate at the courthouse the next morning. Smith would have an opportunity to attack as he moved between the police van and the back door of the building. We assumed his killer would want to remain alive and free to work again and did not have to factor in the appeal of religious martyrdom, which is a more recent and cynical tool of terror."

Mack leaned back, sliding forward on the hard seat to straighten the affected leg at the hip. There was no sign on his face that it bothered him.

"Louis suggested it would be feasible," he said, "to set up a rifle in a window or on the roof of a building overlooking the courthouse entrance. We committed to the idea; there was no time before the event to try anything else. If we were wrong, we would fail. We used the remaining light of dusk and climbed every building that gave a suitable line of sight. Just before sunset, we found it at the second to last possibility. The pigeons gave it away. Rusty's backup sniper did not relish lying prone in pigeon shit. He had prepared a clean spot on a roof with a perfect view of the entrance."

"So you got him!" Skosh did not realize he'd been so caught up in the story until he heard his own voice.

Mack had no time to answer. Charlie came through the door under the staircase, turned on the bright overhead lights, and headed straight for Skosh's no longer invisible corner.

In that instant, Skosh decided against all comfy chairs during an op. By the time he got out of this one, Charlie hit him in the chest with a bloody set of documents.

"Two wallets, two passports, and a US Senate staff ID card," said Charlie. "We'll expect full payment on the intelligence."

Steve stepped up behind him. "All the IDs are Russian-made, except maybe the Senate one. The guy was too proud of his day job and not all that smart. The names are fake, again, except for the Senate card, so I took fingerprints." He handed over two sheets of hotel stationery.

"This is blood." Skosh's eye twitched involuntarily.

"Yeah. It was the only thing available to make a print with. It came from the man the Smiths were calling boss. The other one broke his neck slipping on the bathroom floor."

THIRTY-NINE

C hristine needed to understand this evidence. She stepped up to the three men at the corner chair and pulled on Skosh's hand to see the fistful of documents he had taken from Steve.

"Which one's dead?" she asked. "Paul Smith? Or the one he was working for? Or the one I saw in the park?"

She had a full glimpse of the bloody prints before registering their silence. She looked up to see shock in

Skosh's wide-open eyes, narrowed suspicion in Steve's, and bemusement in Charlie's half-smile.

"I can't help it," she said. "I'm a cop." *It's in my bones.*

A crime, or a gaggle of them, a conspiratorial theater of crimes among criminals, had flipped a switch. She was all in, and it didn't matter that she couldn't trust these guys. Hell, she never trusted the Feds, either, but had always effectively worked with them.

Mack stepped up with the same suppressed amusement as his son. He politely held out his hand, asking Skosh for the documents. The man was always polite, Christine noticed. So polite that after a glance, he offered them to her. Like she was now in partnership with a bunch of hoodlums.

She stared at the passport photos. No enlightenment there. Then there was the staffer ID, with a different name than either of the passports.

"Is one of these guys the Russian from the consulate you've been talking about?" she asked.

Charlie gave an answer, again as if she deserved one. "No." He pointed to the passport picture that did not match the ID. "This one is the boss referred to by the Smiths."

"And he's dead? And those are his prints?" She indicated the bloody papers still in Mack's hand.

"Yes. They're both dead."

"Is the other one the Russian guy?"

"No."

She stared at the ID card in her hand. "The Senate is pretty high up there, I mean, power-wise. Please tell me they're just pretending. It's got to be a deception."

With the barest imitation of a shrug, Charlie said, "Could be. Probably not."

"You're saying a foreign intelligence outfit has a hold on somebody extremely well-placed in our government?"

"Had. He's dead. And yes. Of course."

Mack and Charlie both smiled at her. It was almost warm.

"Why? How?" She sputtered the words.

"Because he was well placed," said Mack. "There is no sense in working to turn a restaurant dishwasher."

"Unless the restaurant is popular with the well-placed," said Steve. "How it's done is simple. Sex, money, or both until you've got enough for blackmail."

Skosh chimed in. "You might add a dose of ideology—delusional before the turn or for the sake of the conscience after—but it's not a requirement. I'd better get to the Consulate to check these prints. I'll be back before breakfast."

"I can probably get them faster through police channels," said Christine.

"But not as secure. He was well enough placed that a simple public disclosure would be a payoff for them. Destabilization is the *aim* of the game." Skosh waved the documents at her, smiling like he was proud of his wit. "Breakfast will be here soon. I'll send Jade over before I leave."

Charlie told Rimas to go upstairs and sleep. It was an order.

So they know about the triangle, thought Christine. And they disapprove.

...

The morning of, thought Jade. In two years, she had learned the rhythm of a Charlemagne operation. They operated mainly in the dark. This one would be in daylight, a bright, hot, sunny day in a major city. But the lead-up was the same, inaugurated by breakfast this time. The scrambled eggs were going fast. The poutine, full of its comfy carbs, sat congealing in its tub on the counter. To be fair, Frank did take two helpings. Skosh put a spoonful on his plate when he came back from the Consulate. *Only to please me.* She could eat the whole tubful but skipped it in favor of the new dress she would buy for the wedding. *Only to please him.*

Rimas came down the stairs, hair sticking up at the back, eyes red-rimmed, jaw set. *Tell him.* This ran through her brain like an endless loop, along with *How?*

Private exchanges of words in various languages came short and at a murmur. The team concentrated on taking in protein and clearing out thoughts of a tomorrow they might not have. One pair, though, rehashed yesterday, and Jade got to hear their conversation because it was at the coffee machine and, surprisingly, in English.

Mack was being polite to Jade. He and Rimas were in her territory, where she kept breakfast going and the all-important morning, noon, and night beverage. He stood on that bad leg without support from cane or counter when Rimas approached with a sullen face.

"What happened? I must know," said Rimas.

Mack shrugged, minimal to be sure, but unmistakable. "She died. But you knew that already."

"I want to know how. And was Harry the sleeper?"

Mack shook his head. "Harry was undisciplined and incompetent, but he lived. Frank's office dismissed him when we complained. But Rusty's people noticed him—sloppy tradecraft is worse than none at all—and that led them to us. Rusty recognized the opportunity of taking out Vasily Sobieski."

"But Antoine? Who was Antoine?"

Another shrug. "Rusty's recruit. A Canadian policeman, a rising star among the Mounties."

"You stopped him, didn't you?"

Mack gave a slight nod. "Only just."

There may have been more, and Jade wanted to know the whole story, but she was pulled away when a bald man came upstairs from the basement. Behind him, Sergei had a hand on his shoulder, directing him to where they stood. He handed the man a plate. Jade gave him the large spoon beside the tub of poutine, and to her intense gratification, he filled the plate.

Empties were returning to the counter, stiff-backed chairs scraped the floor, forming a semi-circle from the computer to the sofa, with Charlie's easy chair as the focus. Jade recognized the beginning of a meeting, probably the last one before Alcoa's speech. Mack took only coffee with him to the sofa.

Rimas picked up a plate and the spoon next to the eggs.

They had as much privacy as any other moment in time was likely to give them.

No time like the present. Keep it simple.

"Rimas, I'm going to marry Skosh."

FORTY

R imas could not swallow anything, least of all this. How did he get her so wrong? Had he been delusional like Vasily? Was she playing false? Was it her fault? He wanted it to be her fault. Blame would staunch the wound. Skosh had placed a chair to the right of Michael. That was a good place for blame, only a couple of meters away, easily crossed. With speed.

How could he lose her to a fucking babysitter?

He had to admit, as he watched his thoughts and emotions speed by his mind like an old-fashioned newsreel, Skosh's skills were respectable.

He put the plate he had been holding down on the counter and assessed his chances. Height and reach were comparable, but Skosh had weight. He also had a lot of formal eastern training. It made him move differently in defense. Rimas had burning anger—always an effective fuel for attack. He felt Misha's attention from the sofa behind him. Maybe he imagined it, but the thought paused his anger, and he turned, glaring with defiance. This was all Misha's doing. He was sure of it.

Reluctantly, he sat chin up and scowling, the cords in his neck taut with simmering fury, in the space Misha indicated on the sofa next to him. "I must know how Gloria died." He murmured it sideways to the culprit next to him.

Michael was beginning the meeting. The last formal meeting for this op. For some, maybe, the last meeting ever.

174

"Vasily shot her." Misha's voice was also at a murmur, covered by the activity around them as people settled into their seats.

"I'm not going to shoot Jade. I love her. I'm going to shoot Skosh." He hazarded a surreptitious glance to the side. Was Misha smiling?

"You love your idea of her," said Misha, "not the woman herself, or you would see a life with us would crush her." Rimas turned to face him, trying to glare but too confused to focus. Misha continued, "And you will not shoot him, or you would have done so already. The crisis has passed, Rimas, and you have done well."

How could it have passed when he was still in such turmoil? He opened his mouth to let loose a torrent of questions, but the room became suddenly silent as Michael began speaking from his corner armchair.

"Let me formally introduce Cody Johansen." He nodded to the bald young man sitting next to Christine, holding a plate filled with a third helping of poutine. "He has given his parole, as they say, and is cooperating to keep his cover and for the sake of breakfast. Please respect that."

A bit light-hearted for Michael, thought Rimas. He must have a plan.

Cody smiled. "The food is first-rate. Thank you."

The remark sank into silence. His mother kicked his foot. Michael, deadpan and with a pointed look at him, said, "I repeat, Cody's cover is imperative."

There were preliminaries. Michael started with a plan for leaving, appointing those who would move lockers of equipment, baggage, and Sergei's computer.

Cody volunteered to help. His mother kicked him again, not for the last time.

The lad had much to learn, thought Rimas.

Steve reported that the team's Challenger jet had landed and was standing by at Mirabel. Another dagger of jealousy for Rimas to parry. Steve's wife, Claire, would be flying them home. Those that lived.

"Why is Michael so relaxed?" he asked Misha in a low voice. He was looking for good news, anything to fill the void of emptiness the last thought had left in him.

"He has let go. It is the only way to face chaos. Without fear, without illusion. He is open." Misha left the low sofa as he spoke, standing to command attention.

"If I may interrupt."

Michael gave a near nod.

...

Christine wondered, was it age that made Mack keep bringing up the past? Would it help? He began with his gaze locked on Frank, who returned the stare with a slow blink of acquiescence over his prominent old eyes. That's right, she remembered, they go back that far. He must remember it well.

She nodded when Mack turned to her. She was listening.

"I have been asked again what it is an intelligence professional uses to turn an asset or agent. How can a person be persuaded to betray his or her most cherished loyalties? The answers are as many as there are people on earth, but they can be described in generalities. As Steve has explained, sex and money are the most potent motivators. Once these have been established in a target's life, they become enforcers as well, in the form of blackmail.

"Then there are those who adopt a philosophical perspective. They ally themselves with the adversary, either ideologically to begin with or as a rationalization afterward.

"But the essential thing to remember is that an operative like Rusty would not waste time and effort to turn an agent without position. Such a target must have access to useful information and influence."

Misha was studying Christine's reaction. She could not help it that her face paled, but her gaze did not waver. She nodded again to acknowledge.

"As it was when we were here in 1971," he continued, "Rusty's backup specialist is a sleeper, an unknown among those tasked to protect the target."

"Which one?" She whispered it.

"My money's on Eric," said Cody. All eyes swiveled to him.

"Why?" Charlie asked it, but everybody wanted to know.

"Because the guys I came upriver with liked him. They thought he was badass because he's heavy into the border patrol identity, but they weren't afraid of him."

"What about John?" asked his mother with a fond smile at the blond fuzz now covering his head as he shook it.

"No. John's a small-town cop from New Hampshire. What's he gonna do for Rusty? Hand out speeding tickets to the target?"

"You have your sleeper," said Mack, addressing Charlie specifically. "A young federal officer with a budding career. In 1971 we had only telltale pigeon shit. But still, it should have been enough. We squandered it."

Now Mack made a pointed surveillance of each member of his audience, pausing longest to lock eyes with the triangle, Rimas especially, and then with Sergei.

"We meant to be and should have been several hours earlier concealed on that rooftop. Our watchers were in position, but we were late. The woman Gloria..."

He paused. Christine heard mortified annoyance in the way he spoke the word woman. Twice.

"The woman, Gloria, met us in a coffee shop next to our new hotel. I asked Vasily if he had told her where we were staying. He shook his head. I should have acted then because I knew and I was responsible. He should have been alert to the danger, but he smiled and approached to kiss her, only pausing momentarily as she reached into her handbag with a troubled scowl.

"She should have fired through the bag. She would have had a chance then, a chance to succeed. She had no chance to live either way. Both Louis and I were in motion, but Vasily was the fastest. Illusion finally deserted him, and he met the threat the way he had always done."

Mack looked at Frank, who closed his eyes and bowed his head. Pieces of this history began to fall into place for Christine.

Frank continued the story. "The gendarmes were everywhere. They wanted your hide, all of you, but especially Sobieski. My in-country contact was God knows where. I had no ID on me. All I had was Harry. He pulled your ass out of the fire, Mack, not me. But I fired him anyway because of the bug in the safehouse. Rusty had us in view all along."

Mack grimaced. "We reached the door onto the roof just as the van opened at the courthouse entrance below us. Rusty's backup, cover name Antoine, lost concentration when he heard our steps. He turned suddenly, rifle and all, finger in the guard, squeezing already but no longer against his target. The first round sliced a television antenna to my left. The second embedded itself in the door frame to my right."

Mack pointed to a faint scar on his cheek.

"A splinter split opened the skin and I bled. Vasily pushed ahead of me from behind. I saw his expression, full of remorse and failure. He thought I had been hit in the face. The first shot from his Makarov made the sniper spin toward the right, sending one more round our way. It hit the masonry of a chimney a few feet from the door, changed its trajectory, and entered Vasily's liver."

He closed his eyes in a long blink. "The Canadian doctors were more than competent. Vasily lost only a portion of his liver and was warned to avoid alcohol, which was no hardship for him. But it was a high cost for the closest we ever came to failure, and Rusty was not responsible for that near disaster; we were."

"I had a helluva time getting you out of here," said Frank. "The authorities tried to confiscate the weapons. The Frenchman was livid."

Christine sat back in her chair, looking up at Mack, wide-eyed. "Eric has become a friend of mine. He is talented and passionate about our rights. You're telling me he's lying, and if I don't believe it, you'll fail?"

Charlie answered, shaking his head. "We won't fail. You will. We are not bodyguards. Our commission is to discover the American funding behind this operation and take out any killers. We have the intel and will finish this afternoon. We will respect your request to stay outside the theater perimeter. The Smiths are still the main threat we were hired to eliminate. But you will have inside with you an armed double agent with a commission from his true supervisor. We think we know which one it is but cannot help you if we are not there. Of course, he will not escape us as he leaves, but you will have failed to protect Alcoa."

Christine appreciated the forthright effort to make her understand. She rubbed her temples. It was a tell, and it was becoming a bad habit.

"Then you will not help us." She could not keep a note of bitter accusation out of her voice. How had she fallen into the trap of thinking a criminal ally could be honorable?

Charlie responded with a slow blink and strained patience. "I understand your need for agency and control, Christine, given your history. But in this instance, it comes with risky decisions that only you can make. Under your arrangement, Eric will kill Alcoa, then die when we see him step outside the perimeter."

"But we're not sure it's him!" She said it with some heat.

"I'm sure, Ma," said Cody.

She kicked him again, but half-heartedly. After taking a moment to rub her temples again, she sighed and said to Charlie, "Isn't there another option?"

Charlie glanced at his father, and Misha said, "I am a more attractive target than Sydney Alcoa. If I am inside when whichever of your deputies decides to shoot, he will start with me, giving you time to protect Alcoa."

"You're willing to be a target?"

He dipped his head to one side in a near shrug. "I have always been a target. I make only one stipulation. Vasily died a decade after our Montreal operation, living out his favorite fantasy that he was not what he was. I have no such illusions. He went to a business meeting unarmed. I will not do that."

Christine studied him as she reviewed the situation before her. The offer was enormous. Sure, he was fit, except for the leg. He moved like a cat—when he moved at all, that is. Was he fit enough? What if this guy died just to salve her conscience with proof it was Eric? It was probably Eric. She looked at the stoney faces around her, waiting.

She remembered the blood she had walked through, the corpse at the door, his neck open. That was not done by Rimas. He shot the other guy. She looked at Mack. Was he skilled enough? *What a stupid question.* Christine turned to Charlie. "My screening plan is solid. I'll need a way that looks natural to get him in with whatever weapon he needs.

Charlie raised a half smile and gave a near nod, his eyes on Fluffy.

FORTY-ONE

Christine took her position stage right and waited for the audience to settle. Sydney Alcoa was still greeting people at the front of the crowd, bending low to shake hands as far as he could reach.

It was not a large park, but they had filled it to capacity and more. She estimated a hundred and fifty people lounging on blankets or folding chairs with only a nod given to the organizers' attempt to mark out rows for ease of movement. It didn't matter. Those who needed to move were accommodated by people in their path with good-natured bustle as they stepped over and around each other.

The space was a grassy bowl facing a flat area with an awning and a curved ten-foot wall behind, where they had set up a low portable stage and an adequate sound system. Alcoa had already been fitted with a mic to be activated when he began his remarks.

Christine scanned the upper edges of the twenty-foot high bowl before her, a 270-degree arc, gently sloping to the two entrances on either side of the stage where her deputies, Eric and John, wielded security wands, denying entrance to any weapons but their own and those of the other three grim-faced men out of the Yukon, well-armed and capable. These had ranged themselves along the back edge of the crowd, watching. Why, she had demanded of Charlie, why couldn't it be one of them? He reminded her Rusty would not waste energy recruiting somebody who earned his livelihood tracking caribou through the wilderness. Behind them, beyond the steep backside of the bowl, Charlemagne held vigil concealed, she surmised, in plain sight.

The last arrivals were late by design. A dark-haired young woman wearing a designer blouse and skirt carried Fluffy in her arms. Her ostensible father, an older man walking with a limp and a cane, escorted her.

Christine crossed the space in front of the stage and reached Eric before he finished checking Jade.

"It's okay, Eric. These are the friends I mentioned."

As Eric finished running the security wand over Jade, Fluffy growled at him from her arms. Mack stood behind her, very dapper in a dark suit, white shirt, and tie. He stood straight, the cane held loosely in his left hand. Wrong hand for the hip.

"You said no exceptions." Eric's tone accused. His eyes strayed continually to the man with the cane, the right one blinking rapidly, brought back only reluctantly to engage hers."

"I know," she said, "but we're running late and need to get started."

Fluffy growled again, and it began.

…

Chatham woke well-rested that morning and not even hungry. The boss's pizza had quelled the memory of the slugs. He was forgiven, else why would the boss leave him this safehouse, complete with food?

He consulted his backpack. The Luger was dirty, and he was out of patches and solvent because the bottle leaked. It was inadequate for the task, anyhow. Slava had said to always make a splash. Needs to be big. Headlines and crisis. That was how he put it in his strange way of talking. A very great man was Slava.

Chatham was glad he never ditched the AK. Sure, it added weight, but it wasn't like he carried anything else. An AK-47 with a folded stock fit nicely in a mostly empty backpack.

He knew he was beginning to smell. Maybe. Well, it was all the same to him. So what if he had a beard? He checked his magazines, inserted one, and chambered a round. It was a little risky with it on his back like that, so he checked the safety. Taking it off would be quieter than chambering, so the risk was necessary. He needed to get going. He hadn't even settled on his approach yet.

…

John stood at the lesser-used entrance to the bowl, the one approached from the back of the park. He had a wand but barely used it. What was up with Eric? When he asked him where the hell he'd been all night, all the guy would say was he needed to walk around to quell the jitters. But he didn't have any jitters. Steady as a rock, over there on the other entrance, except, of course, for the twitch in his eye. John had managed to tell Christine about it but wasn't sure she took it in There was only a nod and an order to watch outward, not in. The Yukon guys will take care of the inside, she said; you watch the approaches to that side.

What about somebody climbing that slope behind those guys? He stepped outside when he saw the bushes move, then turned his head to catch Christine's eye, but she was at the other entrance, out of his line of sight. It couldn't have been more than a nano-second, and he felt the presence before he fully turned back, but by then, the guy was upon him.

…

Paul Smith woke up in his car, blinking in the sunlight. He reviewed his life. The prospect of imminent death will do that to you. He held on to a few things, like love of his mother, respect for his father, childhood good times growing up in the Colorado compound, dawn over Lake Champlain, those kinds of things. But other things had become dust, and more began to crumble from underneath. *What if she isn't a spawn of Satan? What if I am? What if everything is a lie?*

He had always been proud of his warrior status. Special. Fierce. Now, faces paraded across his interior vision, first hers, then others, some brown, most white. Why? That one had to go, didn't he? A nasty guy, right? Sure, all of them. No question. The end times required it. But doubt suddenly engulfed him. He saw clearly what he was, an expendable fool, and what he had to do now. Ironically, he would obey one of his dead boss's orders, but for a different reason.

He started the car, left the box store parking lot where he had taken refuge, and headed toward the park.

...

Michael spotted Paul Smith entering the park, heading toward the back, behind the outdoor theater. He alerted Sergei with a signal to watch. Acknowledged. All thoughts of their loss, nephew and son and grandson, were subsumed under the present exigency, but fear for the stillborn child's mother niggled him and must be tearing at Sergei. *When will we know?* He shoved it aside and hoped Sergei would do the same. Damn the woman and her decision. He wanted to force her to live, realized where his mind was drifting, and forced it back instead, to the outside perimeter of an outdoor theater in a Montreal park.

Skosh's voice on the network: "Found the watcher, one of Yannick's, who made the initial sighting after dawn. He said the guy looked rough, like he's been

living on the street. He carried a backpack. Disappeared into the park. The watcher didn't see him come
out, but he could have left on the other side."

"What about the watchers on that side?" said
Michael.

"They saw nothing."

"Steve?"

"Ours saw no movement until around nine
o'clock," said Steve, "and accounted for all entrances
and exits until the theater was set up."

So Chatham was inside. He would know Charlemagne was there. No matter how carefully they
moved, this guy would be aware, and he wasn't moving. Concealed somewhere. In a patch of trees? Among
those bushes? In the undergrowth behind that gazebo
in the far corner? He would be noticeable among the
bright, happy population, and he would have to move
eventually.

With the thought came a word in his ear from Rimas. A very quiet "Maybe."

So he was headed for the other entrance.

Michael's hand signaled Sergei. Trade places.
Michael studied his movement, looking for signs of
emotion in those light eyes as they met his. None. The
man was steady. It helped Michael maintain his own
center.

He took his new position in time to see Paul
Smith's careful approach from the gazebo in the back
corner of the park. So Chatham wasn't hiding there, or
he's already dead thanks to Paul, vindicating Misha's
uncharacteristic act of mercy.

...

Paul Smith carried his training into the battleground with heightened awareness of his surroundings as usual and now also of himself, a killer and nothing more, with his knife concealed in his hand by his side, bent on silent murder. He was surrounded by others like him, all of them enemies. He sensed them in every good hiding place. He would die as a member of the elect. The question he could not answer was whose elect?

...

Last night's pizza deserted him, and hunger brought Chatham back to unreality, a state that had become more frequent. He knew where he was. In combat. What he didn't know was when.

All these open spaces meant a settlement. It meant the Serb army. There was a sentry. He needed food, but if he fired, the Serbs would hear it. He unfolded the stock of the AK but left the safety on and didn't like to use the knife. All that blood.... He ran to the objective, swinging the AK by the barrel.

...

Rimas put a quiet bullet into Chatham as he moved like a jaguar onto Christine's deputy at the back entrance. Disadvantages of a weak charge, he thought. The man was still attacking. The remedy was exact placement, especially when the target moved erratically. Louis would have done better, would have hit a lethal spot. Rimas adjusted.

"Wait," said Michael in his ear.

Obedience was automatic, and Rimas watched from less than ten feet as the two men, in a death roll in the dust of the entrance pathway, were joined by a third. He could see the glint of a blade in this one's hand, recognized the man they had trussed up in that duplex, and wondered if he should take him out. But the man was defending Christine's deputy. This was not the deputy they suspected, was he? Not the sleeper? Maybe Paul Smith was mistaken. Maybe they were.

"Hold," said Michael, out loud and in the clear, as he approached.

At the same moment, the struggle on the ground ended, blood spreading into the surrounding dust, two of three bodies panting in exhaustion.

Michael pulled up the topmost man and took the knife out of his hand. Rimas rolled the dead man off the deputy and helped him up. Then came the sound of a scuffle at the other entrance and Christine's voice. "John, call an ambulance."

FORTY-TWO

Misha took his place in the crosshairs. He exaggerated the limp as he approached the young man, watching his eyes register recognition, the right one twitching rapidly. *At least I am aware; Vasily was not. I will have the advantage.* He switched attention to the lad's hands. He had cheated death so many times in his long career that it did not increase his anxiety to be acting as the enemy's target. His sole concern was for his son.

If things went wrong and produced disaster, Michael would forever feel the weight of his choice to use his father as bait. It would color all future decisions, even as that missing piece of Vasily's liver had affected his. Maybe it made his judgment more effective; he didn't know. It did mean he would never let one live. Until now, when the narrowed responsibilities of retirement gave him the option.

He hoped Michael would be different.

And what if he was mistaken and Paul Smith's crumbling ideology stood firm? Funny how the most significant test of Misha's reputation for judgment rested on an instant of not killing.

He studied Eric's face, hoping to see another opportunity to decide for instead of against, but Fluffy's snarling crescendo confirmed what Misha saw. The dog stretched his neck, all teeth bared, aiming for the young man's face while straining to escape Jade's firm grasp.

Eric's right hand reached the holster on his belt. He was swift and had it out of the holster with practiced fluidity, but a momentary flinch at the threat from a small dog gave Misha more time than he needed. His hand was practiced, accurate, and silent.

Misha put his knife away while the two women gasped.

Fluffy stopped growling.

...

At least they hadn't executed an innocent man. Christine had seen it herself. She grieved but was at peace with the necessity.

She had been watching Eric's face, saw it settle into a determined snarl as he drew his S&W semi-auto out of the holster on his hip, eyes on Mack. The barrel barely cleared it. The gun fell by gravity, preceding his body to the cinder gravel of the entrance by only a fraction of a moment.

So fast. So silent. Except for Fluffy's noise. Her mouth hung open as she watched Mack pull out a handkerchief to wipe a smear of blood from his wrist. He had already stowed the knife... somewhere.

The beautiful young man she had enjoyed having on her team lay dead at her feet. He had been so confident, so careful to hide his underlying insecurity, always betrayed by his right eye. Maybe he would have overcome it eventually. Of course, he had made his own decisions, but who helped him make this one? With that thought, she reorganized her future. There was a mother somewhere who had just lost her son.

...

Paul reached for the door handle almost before he stopped running. Focused and out of breath, he did not see the tall Asian man until he spoke.

"I wouldn't if I were you."

Paul's hand stopped inches from freedom. His hope sank and the adrenaline drained. He turned to face this muscular new opponent and realized he was at a disadvantage. Again.

"Who the hell are you?" he said, needing the name of this executioner.

"I'm a Fed from the Deep State, and I advise you to get the fuck out of here ASAP. Don't use your car. Don't go home. They know you killed Chatham."

"I was under orders. They'll know that," said Paul, confident the man was lying. It had only been ten minutes. They couldn't know, and the boss would... He remembered the blood in the hotel room.

"How do they know?" he asked suspiciously. He tilted his head back to make eye contact. The man was too tall, too close, and too ready.

"Let's just say someone told them. You'll need this." The Asian held out a thick envelope. Curiosity made Paul take it from him against his better judgment. He opened it.

"Who do I owe now?" he asked, looking up from a fistful of hundreds, both Canadian and U.S.

No answer.

"Why am I alive?" *And how the hell did they disappear so fast?* It was now twelve minutes since the blond man took his knife from him and shoved him toward the park exit. When he had turned to look back, he saw only Chatham dead on the ground, heard the sound of a siren, and took the chance of survival on offer. He ran to his car.

The tall man shrugged and said with a note of urgency, "There's a card with a phone number in the envelope. The message is—these words exactly—if you live and when you think you're safe enough, call." He paused. "Think about it. Those are my words."

Paul crossed the border in a forest after dark, hungry but thoughtful, and headed east. Every step brought him more questions resurrected out of answers he had thought were settled. His former friends were now enemies, his most firmly established belief system in shreds because of a pair of brown eyes.

...

Frank pulled the old car into a bumpy clearing in an expansive forest of mostly maple and pine. He checked the satellite map Sergei had given him, pretty sure he was in the right place. Over there, on the right, it should slope down to a stream. It did.

"Okay, kid, we're here. You got everything?"

"What do you mean everything? A knife and a granola bar? Yeah. I got it." Cody held them up for Frank.

He noticed the blond fuzz on the lad's head was already long enough to suggest it might curl. His third son had been like that. None of the others were as blond. He sometimes wondered….

"I don't even get a map?" demanded Cody.

"You have a compass, and I showed you how to use it. You also know how to use your wits, or you wouldn't be alive after that boat ride."

"Those guys back there are why I'm alive. Them and my mom. My wits would have made me worm food otherwise. I get that I'm in debt to them. This is a helluva way to rub it in."

Frank sighed and switched to a little grandfather mode mixed with case officer. "Remember where you're going. You'll be contacted once you're in place to start your training. After you've been taught a little tradecraft, you'll have the skill to contact your mom. We'll tell her you're okay in the meantime."

Cody surveyed the dense woods before him, listened to the sound of a stream, and saw the underbrush move under an unknown animal. "You're not going to know I'm okay until I get through all this, cross the border, get through more of it, and find a phone, so anything you tell her now will be a lie."

The kid had a future, thought Frank, but one thing at a time. "We'll know, Cody. Don't forget, you've escaped. You have your legend memorized. Don't stray from it. The more this little jaunt takes out of you, the better the legend sounds, so don't clean up. We'll be in touch."

He watched Cody jump the creek and disappear under the canopy of trees. Cody didn't know it, but he was already in training.

The bottom of the jalopy scraped the tops of ruts in the soft ground as Frank shifted to first and headed toward the road to Mirabel. He wondered what he would meet at the team's jet. How many bodies, and in what shape?

FORTY-THREE

Skosh had not seen this before. Not even a scratch on any of them. All hale, but not so hearty. They schlepped equipment without energy. Going through the motions of going home. Going home to a tragedy.

Two of their own were casualties. Two who hadn't even been on the most spectacular untying of a true goat rope Skosh had ever seen the team accomplish. No shots fired in a summertime crowd of 150 people, all of them sorry the nice young man at the entrance had a medical emergency but glad to hear a speech by a great man, even if it was a little delayed.

At the airplane, no celebration was possible. One had died before his first breath; the other was still a question mark. Wait and see, their chief pilot, Claire, had murmured when he asked her about Mara as she unlocked the baggage compartment.

Frank pulled up next to him at the airplane and handed him the keys to the babysitters' car.

"Jade and I are taking the car back to the States, Frank. We could have taken Cody to his starting point on our way. The team's inside waiting for you. None too patiently, I imagine."

Frank gave him a crinkled smile. "I had team business, Skosh. Happy to do it. Charlie knows. You should take the Mercedes back. It's much more comfortable."

"And have you guys listening to everything we say? No thanks."

Another, broader smile this time, from an old man with a grey fringe around his shiny scalp, not as chubby as he used to be, but every bit as sharp. The look in those prominent eyes set Skosh's mind in motion, like a train with no brakes. He remembered the babysitters' car was equally bugged and had been since the beginning.

"So Frank," he said, meeting that smile with a scowl, "Charlie's got plans for those two—Cody and his mom—doesn't he? He's creating another network, isn't he?"

Frank patted his arm. "You always were a pro, Skosh." Take the Mercedes. Your fiancée deserves the treat.

...

Rimas stared through the window, contemplating the clouds below as evening light faded over the North Atlantic. Reason helped him deal with the anger. He had to admit Skosh was an excellent babysitter. The team needed him. For survival.

The memory of Christine became another aid, a curated memory stripped of any illusionary future. It opened a new compartment in the rubric of his life: valued occasional lover. There might be another opportunity with her, but the meantime still stretched empty before him.

"Hey, partner." Steve took the seat across from him when Sergei fell into a troubled sleep across the aisle. Rimas responded with a tired smile.

"Danny's going back to college in a few days," said Steve. "There's something I need to do for him before he goes, after the baby's funeral is over, and I'm wondering if you want to help."

Danny was Steve's son, a formidable teenage fighter but untried because his father insisted on education first. Rimas raised an eyebrow. Go on, it said.

"There's a place I know about," said Steve, "on the other side of a particular mountain. Louis and I and Louis's uncle Bertrand used to visit occasionally— make that frequently— before I was married. Nice place. Reasonably safe. Thought you might want to go. Maybe you can keep an eye on Danny for me in the future, too. The Spare is still too young to go with him.

Rimas had never been to a bordello. Christine had opened his eyes to the extent of his ignorance of women. He refused to call it innocence because he was almost thirty, for heaven's sake. "Education is a valuable thing," he said, matching Steve's broad smile.

...

Michael poured a generous dram of single malt into a glass and handed it to his father before sitting in the facing seat.

"Claire says Theresa has been sending updates every hour, Papa. We'll know more before we land." Misha closed his eyes as he swallowed the entire liquid fire at once, feeling its warmth descend to his core. When he opened his eyes again, Michael was watching him.

"I never mention these things to Alex," said Michael. His tone was reassuring.

"She does not control me." He clipped each word, not hiding his peevishness, and saw Michael fight a threatening smile. Why did no one take him seriously on this issue?

195

"You will need to be careful in your handling of Damon Kowalski, Michael. It is a major shift for him, and he will have more enemies now, especially among the Smiths."

Michael nodded. "Frank is aware of it. No better man to set up an American network for the coming struggle, I think. Provided his health allows it."

The word health fell heavily between them, and Michael refilled both glasses, not saying the name Mara, at the center of both their thoughts. It overshadowed for a moment the heavier, more personal concern nagging at Misha's mind.

He had let one live, and so had his son.

EPILOGUE

Skosh had been seated at this table two years before, facing the same three critics: his boss, his boss's boss, and the slimy ass-kisser from another section he knew only as Seeker. He suspected Seeker was responsible for the urgent summons that forced him to curtail his honeymoon. His displeasure showed itself only in the still gaze he learned from Mack. It took Seeker a few moments to catch on to the threat. He swallowed and looked away.

Skosh's boss, Bill, opened a file folder and began proceedings."It has been suggested…"

"By whom?" Skosh was feeling reckless.

"That is not material…."

"I'd say it is very material, at least to me. My wife and I were enjoying the fall color in Vermont. The con-do we booked is non-refundable."

"I am concerned," put in the division head, Henry, "that you appear unconcerned about the reason you are here, Skosh."

"That would be because there is no reason."

"You were told..."

"No, I wasn't."

Henry took a deep breath and shuffled through the papers in another folder. "You received verbal counseling in this room two years ago..."

"If it was verbal, why is it in a file?" Skosh raised his eyebrows in question, his face as innocent as he could make it."

"It isn't. Only the fact of the counseling is here, not the subject." Henry's exasperated tone made it clear he was unhappy. Skosh had no problem with that. He liked to share.

"We remember the subject because we were all here," said Henry. "You were counseled not to engage in an intimate relationship where there was the possibility of a power imbalance between you within this organization.

Skosh gave a near nod. He waited, interested to see how they planned to make this into something it wasn't.

"You can't wriggle out of this just by marrying the girl," said Seeker.

Skosh made a plan to alter the smirk on Seeker's face. It began in a dark alley.

"Marriage does negate the problem of a power imbalance," said Bill. "Provided it was not forced...."

"She said 'I do' in accordance with the laws of the state of Virginia," said Skosh. "So did I. We both agreed in front of witnesses. She even bought a new dress for it. We went halfsies on the reception. There are pictures if you need evidence."

"As I was saying," continued Bill after a deep breath, "it negates the reason you were verbally counseled, but there is still the additional problem of nepotism posed by this allegation."

"She doesn't work for me."

"She runs your library."

"As an employee in a separate administrative division. And I didn't hire her or even recommend her."

"You have been taking her as an assistant on your operations."

"She was recommended by personnel two years ago. We had never met."

"Come off it, Skosh," said the slimeball, Seeker. "You don't expect us to believe you never took advantage of her on any of those ops?"

Skosh let his gaze linger an extra beat before deciding on his attack. First, the nepotism charge. He and Jade both wanted to keep their jobs. Next, the destruction of a known enemy. The best way would be a political, bureaucratic method, though Skosh had the power and plenty of inclination to make it physical.

He looked at Henry. "Just because we're employed by the same agency doesn't mean we don't have the right to choose who we marry. We were hired and are supervised by different divisions. I'd say as long as the organizational structure keeps me from having any role in my wife's career, and vice versa, there is no nepotism here."

"There's still the matter of your disobeying the counseling," said Seeker with an almost snarl. "You know damn well you didn't leave her alone every time you went out."

"I have to wonder about people who spend a lot of time speculating what goes on in other people's bedrooms. As a husband, I will be sure to remember your insult to my wife, Seeker." He left no doubt of his meaning, but Seeker opened his mouth again to argue, saved only by an interruption from Bill.

"The bottom line, Skosh, is that you are hereby verbally counseled to take no role in the advancement of your wife's career. Specifically, you will not be permitted to take her with you as your assistant during an operation."

Best news ever. Skosh debated pulling a sour face to make them happy that they had somehow hurt him, but the smug look of triumph on Seeker quashed the impulse.

The meeting broke up, and Skosh left the room thinking about dark alleys.

The End

If you enjoyed *Goat Rope*, consider leaving a short review at your favorite bookstore.

Join the Charlemagne Files newsletter for more stories and information about the series, its world of covert operations, and the lives of the characters on the team. Sign up at charlemagnefiles.com/contact.

CHARLEMAGNE AND THE SECTION

The fictional world of The Section follows a few conventions. It may help the first-time reader of The Charlemagne Files to know some of these.

Who/what/ where is The Section?

The Section is a department of an intelligence agency of the United States. Its employees are civil servants. It includes support staff members who provide identity documents, financial controls, and physical and document security. The offices are near the East Coast, maybe Virginia.

The operational agents are called babysitters. They arrange on-site logistical support for freelance specialists during operations. Most operations are not conducted within the United States, with some exceptions.

Babysitters themselves do not carry identity documents in their names during an operation and never carry any official identification from their organization. Their purpose is to allow the organization to deny any association with them or their mission.

Nicknames

Babysitters in The Section receive nicknames from their coworkers when they join the office. These names are often undesirable and used mercilessly among the members of the office. It is part of the team-building process in a stressful occupation.Coins

Challenge coins are traditionally stamped with symbols or mottos that designate the intelligence unit of their owners.

The tradition is that when members of the unit are present at the bar and one produces his coin, all must produce theirs. Anyone failing to show their coin is responsible for the bar tab. If all produce their coins, then the challenger who first produced his or her coin is responsible for the tab.

File designations

The highest classification of information is Top Secret. Beyond Top Secret, more sensitive information is strictly controlled in a number of ways including designation as Sensitive Compartmented Information (SCI). This requires an additional clearance and often a named clearance based on Need-To-Know.

In The Section, files on specialists or specialist teams receive a one-word code name, printed across the file and restricted to very few people. When a solo or specialist team is employed on an operation, another designator word will refer to the operation and will be used for funding, reports, etc.

The Section's file name for Charlemagne is WEDGE. Thus CETUS WEDGE (second book of the Charlemagne Files) means an operation dubbed CETUS using the team called WEDGE.Specialist

A team or solo operative used by Western governments for black operations conducted without fingerprints in high-risk situations expected to involve death.

GLOSSARY OF NAMES

Frank Cardova: long-time babysitter of Charlemagne; later, head of The Section; retired by the time of *Vory*; real name is Leo Vilseck; Section nickname is Buddy.

Rimantas Dockus (Dots-kūs) - called Rimas, protégé of Kestutis, newest member of Charlemagne.

Claire Donovan : deputy chief pilot employed by Charlemagne, married to Steve Donovan.

Steve Donovan: member of Charlemagne; martial artist; former fighter pilot; abandoned real name was Daniel Martin Kessler..

The Frenchman: deceased marksman and technical expert of Charlemagne; real name is Louis; last name is unknown.

Justin Goodwin: FBI special agent and IT specialist; no aliases.

Mack: so dubbed by Western babysitters because he uses a knife at times; leader and decision maker of Charlemagne; called Misha by other members of his team; probable real name is Michael; last name is unknown.

Michael: Misha's son. Game name Charlie.

John Nakamura: official game name. Usually called by his Section nickname, Skosh; successor to Frank Cardova.

Sergei Pavlenko: former KGB agent, now the gadget and explosives expert of Charlemagne. Married to Mara.

Mara Sobieski Pavlenko: computer expert and marksman of Charlemagne. Daughter of Vasily Sobieski, the team's deceased explosives expert. Biological daughter of Misha, half-sister of Michael, married to Sergei Pavlenko.

Alexandra Sobieski: widow of Vasily Sobieski and daughter of former Charlemagne babysitter and head of The Section Fred Dolnikov; no aliases; now married to Mack.

Vasily Sobieski: deceased explosives expert and martial artist whose father was a noted solo specialist; no aliases.

Charlie Taylor: marksman; son of Mack; probable real name is Michael; last name unknown.

Jade Wilmerton - game name of Penelope Prendergast, Chief Administrator of The Section Vault.

www.ingramcontent.com/pod-product-compliance
Lightning Source LLC
Chambersburg PA
CBHW070500260626
47161CB00004B/1396